# Brevité

## A Collection of Short Fiction

Stephen Mustoe

A PEACE CORPS WRITERS BOOK

Brevité
A Collection of Short Fiction

A Peace Corps Writers Book
An imprint of Peace Corps Worldwide



Printed in the United States of America
by Peace Corps Writers of Oakland, California.




ISBN-13: 978-1-935925-75-0

Library of Congress Control Number: 2016939675

First Peace Corps Writers Edition, April, 2016

*For Rhonda, the keeper of my flame*

*Good things, when short, are twice as good.*

*– Baltasar Gracian*

# *Acknowledgments*

This is a collection of stories and poems ranging from thinly veiled memoir to pure fiction. As is true of many writers, I often drew heavily on personal experience. Other times I simply made things up, and had fun doing so.

I am thankful for the encouragement, criticism (sometimes blunt), and suggestions offered by the friends and colleagues who read the many drafts of my stories. Bob Welch and Jane Kirkpatrick, through their leadership of the Beachside Writers Workshops, offered valuable advice and direction. Marian Haley Beil of Peace Corps Writers was a helpful and gracious editor. My biggest fan, my lovely wife Rhonda Stoltz, provided the kicks in the butt I needed at just the right times to keep me from abandoning this endeavor. Her faith in me is amazing, and I am richer for it.

*Dinner for One* was originally published in *The Chaffey Review, a literary journal XII*, Ed. Kimberly B. Johnson and Chris Salazar, 2014.

*Closure* was originally published *in Ten Years After: The Best of Beachside Writers, 2005–2015,* Ed. Roger Hite and Bob Welch, 2015.

An excerpt from *Blind Faith* and an earlier version of *Jack* were originally published in *Inside Beachside: 2013 Beachside Writers' Conference*, Ed. Roger Hite, 2013.

# *Contents*

## *San Blas*

Soft dawn light on milky skin
sweet thick breath upon my face
a murmur as you stretch and turn
pressing close against me

I trace the line of thigh and hip,
the gentle curving of your breast
my eyes drawn to your sleeping smile
– and check the urge to hold you

I rise, walk out past sleeping palms
in morning dew both bright and cool
the pain of loss already sharp,
the wound my own creation

Alone upon the morning sand
losing myself in heat and tequila
I do not sense your soft approach
I'm startled as you sit beside me

# *Closure*

Judging from the height of the sun it was a little after noon. Later than he'd hoped, a sign he was getting old. As he crested the ridge he slowed, then stopped, listening. Nothing broke the silence save the slight whisper of pine needles in the breeze. He felt his pounding heart slowly return to its normal rhythm, tried to ignore the shooting pain in his hip, the ache between his shoulder blades caused by the heavy pack.

Nothing had changed. He had not expected anything to be different, yet felt relieved to find it so. He closed the few yards to a spot where the ground was level, unshouldered his pack, and set to work. A short while later his small tent was pitched, his bag unrolled. He took a sip of water and looked around.

Perhaps twenty yards in front of him the grassy earth fell away precipitously. As he approached the edge the anticipated sense of vertigo licked at his senses. Straight ahead was the rock, her rock, the one she would sit on for hours at a time as she took in the vista below. Two hundred feet below the hillside began to level out a bit, steep still but increasingly less so. Off in the distance, a good four miles or more, was the trailhead. Another ten miles from that lay the town. Nothing at the moment betrayed its existence but he knew that sometime after sunset the lights from the half dozen homes there would shine like shy fireflies, twinkling faintly through the forest.

He nervously sat on the bench-like stone, remembering how she would tease him, how she affectionately made fun of his fear of heights. It was her rock – their rock – only this time she was not with him to enjoy the sense of floating above the landscape below. A familiar feeling of loss crept over him. After a few minutes he carefully stood up and backed away to the safety of his camp.

They had been together a few short months when she brought him here. They had packed light, she insisting they needed nothing more than their bedrolls and a light tarp that late in the season. The mosquitoes were done for the summer and though there was frost in the morning they woke warm, snuggled in their zipped-together sleeping bags. They had made love on the grass the evening before, again that night, once more when they woke wrapped in each other's arms. She couldn't stop smiling. He couldn't stop thinking how much he loved watching her smile.

They were young then, full of the moment, not knowing what to expect of their romance. Had either of them known they would bond so tightly, that they would spend decades intertwining their lives, they might have been more tentative. Instead they threw themselves into each other, filled their days with togetherness, found ways not to be apart. When she needed to relocate for her studies he quit his job to follow her. When he agonized over a risky change in careers she had supported him in ways that surprised and amazed him. Each had been proud and defensive of their independence in past relationships, had left lovers who threatened their autonomy. This time they didn't care, they simply wanted to be together. Always.

He dozed in the late afternoon sun and woke shortly before it disappeared over the horizon. After firing up the small stove he ate sparingly of the meal he had packed that morning: ramen noodles with a can of chicken, her light and simple standby. He had always wanted to bring more substantial fare when they hiked up to this place, she had been adamant that they leave all that behind. At home he was the chef, flattering her with elaborate meals that often took him hours to prepare. In the mountains she ruled the kitchen. He learned to get by on her minimalist cuisine.

He finished his supper, eatıng from the small pot with a bent spoon that was as old as he was. Dessert was a few sips of dark rum from the flask she had given him the first birthday after they had met. Sitting in the glooming dusk, holding the small metal vessel in his hands he again felt the pain of her absence. Tears were forming as he opened the tent and slipped inside. Lying in the warmth of the down bag he tried his best to enjoy this moment of solitude, this pure, clean escape from his everyday world. His mind would not shut off, his thoughts would not stray far from her. Memories fell over one another as they rushed from his consciousness. Sometime long after the stars burned brightly he fell into a troubled sleep.

It was well after sunrise when he awoke. He listened to the sound of a small animal exploring outside the tent, stretched his sore muscles in the shelter of his nylon cocoon. When he could no longer bear to lie still he emerged from the tent, filled the pot with water from his bottle, and set it to boil.

Coffee. Nothing could compare with that first cup, here, at home, anywhere. That was their shared vice, their common addiction. She had been a tea drinker; he had felt triumphant when he finally converted her to the strong black liquid. Since then they had shared thousands of pots of good dark java. Every morning they were together, over the course of nearly forty years, the ritual was the same. He would rise first and bring the steaming cups back to bed with him. Most mornings they would quietly read the paper together, side by side, their legs touching under the covers. Ritual – he spoke the word and was puzzled by its sound, by the meaning it held for most people. Perhaps, he thought, some other word would better describe the special nature of the act, would capture the singular closeness they felt each time they sipped their cups beside each other. No, he realized, there was no better word.

There had been no children. She had surprised him with her decision, explaining carefully how she did not want to share him, did not want their closeness diluted by obligation to offspring. At first he had felt disappointed, later he came to embrace her choice as if he himself had brought it up. There were cats – too many of them over the years – and nieces and nephews who would stay with them on occasion, but nothing or no one to come between them and the love that bound them together. He first used the phrase "joined at the hip" in jest, poking fun at their mutual dependence, their powerful contentedness in a world of two. Over time he could find no finer way to describe their closeness.

He sat on the rock and sipped slowly from his metal cup, dangling his feet off the edge, trying not to think of the airy void below. When the cup was empty he debated whether to fix another. Not this time, he decided, not now. He knew another cup would only help him postpone the dreadful moment, would reinforce the lethargy he felt enveloping him.

He rose, painfully, and walked slowly back to the tent. In his pack was a large container, an ordinary plastic jar that had once held a gallon of some condiment. He was surprised once again by its heaviness. Cradling the object in both arms, holding it close to his chest, he retraced his steps to the rock. It was inexplicably hard going; each step took more effort than he'd expected, as if the jar were gaining weight as he went. He had to force himself to put each foot forward, had to focus on the diminishing distance to the rock. At last he was there, teetering on the edge, trying his best not to look down. This is it, he thought, this is all there is, all there ever will be. He was weeping as he undid the lid, and had to drop to his knees for fear of falling. A deep breath, a concentrated surge of energy, and he was holding the jar in his outstretched arms, pointing to the earth far below, watching as she left him, as what was left of her flowed heavily out of the container and was caught briefly in the breeze wafting up from below.

When it was over he sat sobbing, caressing the empty vessel, astonished at its lightness. It was as if it had never held anything of substance, had always been this void of content. He sat there for a very long time, long after the tears had dried, after his chest had unclenched, after his breathing had returned to normal.

Once he felt able to move again he made his way back toward the tent. Carefully he poured a cup of water from the nearly empty canteen into the small pot. He lit the stove, sat down, and waited for it to boil. One more cup and he would be on his way. Dark strong liquid, almost too hot to drink. A precious treat, something to look forward to every morning of every day of the few remaining years of his life. A ritual.

# *Dogfish Blues*

Uncle Woody hated sharks. Not in a detached, impersonal way; he didn't just find their prehistoric nature or voracious appetite repulsive. He loathed them, abhorred them, despised them with a passion usually reserved for axe murderers, child molesters, or genocidal tyrants. Woody had been a Navy flier in the South Pacific, had survived in shark-infested waters after bailing out of his flaming Corsair. He had stayed awake – and alive – for hours bobbing alone in a vast watery wasteland, his only companions the evil fish that circled round him. It was not something he liked to talk about.

Growing up a stone's throw from Puget Sound I never got to see much in the way of the man-eaters my uncle detested. Though the Seattle Aquarium hosted a few large, reportedly vicious specimens, the most the placid waters of the sound could offer were dogfish – small, relatively benign mud sharks. They were a threat to neither fishermen nor swimmers, were considered by most a mere nuisance. But not Woody. He hated them with the same brutal intensity he harbored toward their larger brethren. It was clear to all that, in his mind, the only good shark – large or small – was a dead one.

Woody loved to fish, and so did I. Many a weekend morning found us drifting a half-mile off the shore somewhere north of Seattle. My uncle may have preferred salmon, but he was quite open-minded about the catch he would bring home. Rock fish, flounder, sea-run cutthroat – as long as it was good eating it found its way into the boat. Woody kept nearly everything he caught. Except dogfish.

The drill was always the same. Whenever one of us would snag a dogfish he would bring it as close to the side of the boat as possible, lifting it out of the water without actually hauling it over the gunwale. The shark, bless its primeval heart, would usually just hang there. If Woody had caught the loathsome creature he would hand over his rod to me at the last moment. Then he would reach into the metal box under his seat, take out his old M1911 Navy pistol, and blow the unfortunate animal away. For a pre-teen boy raised in a gun culture it was fun to be part of this war against the *squalus acanthias* tribe. Sure, some blood and guts might splatter one of us, or perhaps soil the side of the boat, but the important thing was obvious: there was now one less shark in the world.

It was a few days after my twelfth birthday, an early winter morning that was nowhere near as cold as it should have been. Woody had taken me out fishing as a belated birthday present. We were bundled well against the chill, me in a thick wool sweater, Woody in a worn lumberman's jacket that seemed as old as he was. Perhaps it was his way to fend off the chill, perhaps he was just in a celebratory mood, but Woody was sipping from a bourbon bottle all morning. I was used to his quaffing a few beers and getting happy. This morning he was downright euphoric – until he caught the dogfish.

We were going for bottom fish that day, fishing a slack tide, and had a nice catch after only an hour or two. The minute he hooked the small shark Woody knew what he had on the line. Curses that my young ears should never have heard flew from his lips as he fumbled for the box and his sidearm. He almost dropped the pistol as he tried to retrieve it with one hand, then suddenly remembered to pass his pole over to me. I nearly lost my grip on the rod in the awkward transfer, but managed to bring the evil fish slightly out of the water – the same as I had done many times before. This time, however, the shark was not content to dangle off the hook and meet its fate.

Just as Woody was about to squeeze the trigger the dogfish gave a violent flip – and landed inside the boat. Without stopping to think Woody swung his arm around, pointed in the general direction of the writhing creature, and got off two quick shots. Neither shot hit the shark, which was now flopping with increased vigor on the bottom of the boat. Fortunately for me, Woody missed my foot by inches. Unfortunately for both of us he did not miss the boat. A very long pause ensued while Woody took stock of what exactly he had done. He seemed in a trance, studying the dogfish, the two jagged holes in the wood planking, the water oozing in and starting to fill the bottom of the boat. Then, with all the calm deliberation in the world, he looked up at me and said, "Aw shit, Stevie, start bailing."

We nearly made it to shore. I don't know if it was my fear of being in the icy water or the fact that I didn't know how to swim, but I was a dervish with the bailing can. Woody fired up the small kicker motor but it was no use; despite my superhuman bailing efforts we were taking on water fast. When the boat finally sank out from under us we were in shallow water, waist-deep but still a good thirty yards from shore. Woody quickly dragged me out and practically hauled me up the bank to his old GMC pickup, cursing the dogfish and its brothers, sisters, cousins, and long-deceased ancestors. We sat in the cab shivering, waiting for the heater to have some effect, drinking what lukewarm coffee was left in his thermos. Once our teeth had stopped chattering, Woody looked at me, sober as a parson. "Stevie," he said, in a softer voice than I'd heard before, "We can't tell your Aunt Helen what happened to the boat. Promise me you'll tell her we hit some rocks."

It was late afternoon by the time Woody pulled into his driveway. We had sat in the pickup for quite some time pondering just how we would recover the boat. Even at low tide it would be a fair ways from shore, assuming the outgoing tide wouldn't carry it away altogether. Finally my uncle made his decision – to hell with it, just leave the damned boat, it was hardly worth the effort of getting it back. And the motor… well, that was a tough one but after this much time in the salt chuck it was probably beyond resuscitating. May as well just call it a day and go home.

Aunt Helen met us at the door, a puzzled look in her eyes as she took in the salt crust on our faces and the empty boat trailer. "My God, Woodrow, what happened?" "Well, hon, there was this rock we didn't see..." Something in his eyes aroused my aunt's suspicion and she whirled on me. "Okay Stevie, what really happened? Did you hit a rock or did your uncle do something stupid again?"

It was all I could do to muster up a trustworthy expression, to put on my best twelve-year-old stage face. "Yes, Aunt Helen, we really did hit a rock. I swear!" She looked long and hard at me, then rolled her eyes slightly, a grin creeping across her face. "Yes, Stevie, I suppose you did," she chuckled. "Let's get you inside and into some dry clothes. Your uncle can sleep in his damned truck!"

# *Acceptance*

She hunches forward, birdlike, vulturine, fumbling with her cigarette. At the last moment she remembers to slip the oxygen tube from her nostrils, tucks it under her chin before striking the lighter. “I remember the day we brought you home from the hospital,” she croaks. “Your father was so worried he wouldn't drive the Chevy – it was too light – so he borrowed your uncle's Oldsmobile, a big heavy car. Safer. He drove maybe twenty miles an hour, cars behind us were honking. We both were so thrilled....” Her voice tapers off to a whisper as she stares at some indeterminate place, a spot on the table between them. He doesn't reply. He has heard this story before.

“The worst part of growing old,” she tells him, “is the guilt. I wish I could do it all over again, I would have raised you differently, but you were the first, I didn't know. We didn't know.” He sits silently, letting her ramble on. He has heard this before as well. Each time he struggles, thinking he should say something that will comfort her, that will let her know that he understands. He remains mute.

“Your father was a good man,” she sniffles, “we just showed our love in a different way.” His pulse quickens, he wants to correct her, remind her of her lengthy tirades, the nights he spent awake listening to her shrill harping, her fierce berating. He recalls coming home from school, his father's clothes littering the front yard where she'd thrown them. Recalls the beaten look on his father's worn face as he tried to apologize for her. "She's not well, the strokes changed her. We have to allow for that." Yes, he thought, we should allow for that. But he couldn't. He could not get past the way she turned her anger on and off at will, how she could appear so normal so much of the time then slip into frightening viciousness with no warning.

"I'm not afraid of dying," she wheezes. "Not afraid at all – it's my time, I know that. I don't have much longer. I just wish I could make it up to you kids. I wish I could have been a different mother."

So do I, he says to himself, so do I. He thinks of how it would have been to be able to bring friends to the house, to have someone sleep over without witnessing the raging troll that dictated the terms of his adolescent existence. He fantasizes briefly about a mother who would have baked cookies for him and his buddies, laughing with them, who had an interest in what mattered to him at that age – sports, girls, getting his drivers license. He catches himself before the tendrils of sympathy start to pull him off course, begin to dull his anger.

She starts to say something, loses her train of thought. Her head lolls forward in her arms, her cigarette smolders in her gnarled hand. A trickle of drool glistens on her chin. Gently he removes the cigarette, places it in the ashtray beside her, and walks out the back door into the yard. The night is chill; a halo of fog surrounds the full moon. He longs to see the stars but must be content to feel the thick quiet of the night.

He replays a scene that burned itself into his memory decades ago. They are in Arkansas, visiting her kinfolk, gone to the creek to escape the sultry thick heat. He is ten years old, full of fried pies and sweet iced tea. Grandma is asleep on a blanket thrown on the gravel shore. His mother and father emerge from the water, dripping wet, a smile on both their faces. They are holding hands. He will keep this image close in years to come, wielding it as a shield against the anger and pain that resonates throughout the house.

He studies his mother with more care than usual. She seems so insubstantial, a stick figure come to life. The slightest breeze would waft her away, the mildest shock and her shallow breathing would cease. It seems impossible that her thin claw of a hand could ever have held his father's strong, robust one.

His father was a carpenter. He loved his children, he loved her despite herself. He would have liked to have spent more time playing with his offspring, reading to them, watching them grow – but the second jobs, the evening and weekend labors needed to pay her medical bills stole his every spare moment.

Recalling one outing with his father brings him to the verge of tears. It was a Saturday, they had the early hours of the day together before his father had to slip away to work on a remodel project for someone. They were fishing for bass at a lake not far from home. A thin mist rose off the surface, blurring the boundary between water and air. The morning had been slow, but the fish finally started biting. He was excited as he reeled in his first catch of the day, a plump one-pounder that fought right up to the net. Readying his hook for another cast he caught his father looking at his watch. “I'm sorry,” he said. “but we need to wrap things up. I have to drop you at home and go to work. We'll come here again soon, I promise.” The look in his father’s eyes filled him with such sadness he had to quickly glance away. When they got home his mother started right in on both of them. For the first time he envied his father's need to be away from the house. Had he been able to wield a hammer or saw a straight cut he would have pleaded to join him.

She is awake now, slowly reentering the here and now. He asks her if she would like some coffee. “Yes,” she says, “that would be nice.” He gets up to make a fresh pot. As he spoons the grounds into the maker he realizes she is looking at him, tears in her eyes. “I'm so sorry,” she says, and the rest of her words are lost in small sobs and sniffles.

He feels he should comfort her, should let her know it is alright, that she needn't apologize. He tries his best to form the words that will spare her this self-condemnation, struggles to say what he knows he ought to say, what any son facing his dying mother would say.

“Yes, mother, I know you are,” he replies.

## *Encounter*

It was, I told myself, a wonderful day to be alive. One of those crisp mornings that tells you summer is not yet ready to give up. That the most autumn can do for the moment is try for a small toehold. The wall of dark green on either side of me flew past in a blur, interrupted randomly by flecks of yellow, early markers of the season to come. Yes indeed, a wonderful day.

The three of us had swapped lead for the first hour or so, taking turns, waving the trailing riders past when we felt we'd hogged the point position long enough. We'd just crested the low summit, the road upward empty of all but the occasional tumbleweed or pine cone, a conga line of three brightly colored bikes rushing along at well above the speed limit. I was feeling on top of my game, the sleek red machine under me thrumming like a turbine, my thighs a bit tired from clamping the tank up the twisty road to the pass. The sun over my shoulder cast an almost surreal light on the pavement ahead. Matt was in front then and as he backed off the throttle to sweep his helmet camera slowly from side to side I shot by him like he was a Harley in a parking lot. I couldn't help myself –

the sun on my leathers, the smooth snick, snick of the shifter as I dropped two gears to pass, the giddy intoxication of speed, speed, more speed. I reined it in a bit past ninety and focused on the forested corridor ahead. I had at most ten or fifteen seconds before I would be faced with a hard right, just at the mouth of a mountain meadow, a tight curve where the road disappeared from view. I was searching for my braking point, trying to isolate the one spot in the road where I would have to scrub speed and throw my body inward, when I caught a glimpse of movement on the right maybe a hundred feet ahead.

By the time I had backed off the throttle I was nearly abreast of it – a deer, bounding out of the roadside brush. Running toward me, a few feet from contact. Sheer reflex had me bracing. It felt eerily like slow motion, a sense of detachment punctuated by the realization that I was going to die.

And then – nothing. No impact, no painful, deadly change in direction as a hundred pounds of mass intercepted my trajectory. I was already way too hard on the brakes and I felt the rear end slide out as I held on and rode the Ducati away from a high side. As I reached the far shoulder I dropped the bike in the gravel, jumping off at walking speed, shaking uncontrollably. I had to sit down, fast, nausea rising. Confusion overwhelmed me, I was struggling to keep shock at bay.

Matt pulled up behind, jumped off his bike, and ran over to put his arm around me. "God, Jamie, I can't believe you're alive! This is incredible. I have it all on my cam. You won't believe it!"

Believe what? I thought. Belief was not an issue, finding an explanation was. How could I have missed the deer? Point blank at ninety does not leave much wiggle room. I hadn't swerved, hadn't done anything but grab the binders and prepare to wake up dead.

Matt caught me looking back down the road as Rich pulled up alongside of us. "What the hell happened?" he asked Matt. "Why is her bike down, is she okay?"

"Yeah, she's fine," Matt replied. "Not a scratch. Not a scratch on the deer either."

"It jumped right over her."

It took a few days before I could bring myself to watch the video. Finally, sitting in Matt's apartment, my second margarita in hand, eyes glued to his big screen, I let myself comprehend the impossible. The deer, a big buck with a missing antler, his right one, had gone airborne at the exact moment our paths should have intersected. Jumped over me, clean, hadn't even broken stride, continued across the road and disappeared into the underbrush. It was all there, incontrovertible, a miracle borne true. I felt weak.

It was several more days before I could make myself crawl back on the bike, could summon the courage to ride outside the safe environs of the small town I call home. It was ridiculous, I reminded myself. A freak encounter, not something I was ever likely to see again.

Still I rode timidly out a few miles, had a hard time getting any speed up. After a half hour I turned around and headed back to the stable. I still had some recovering to do.

It was late in the day. More than a month had passed since my brush with death. The woods lining the road were no longer mostly green; orange, yellow, and occasional splashes of red flanked the soft gray asphalt ribbon. A lovely fall afternoon, no traffic to speak of, just me and the road climbing steadily upward. I rewound the mental footage, slowed down, identified the place where the incident had occurred. I pulled off the road a bit beyond, parked the bike, and walked back. Looking, examining, hoping for a sign. I found it, a thin line trampled through the tall grass and shrubbery, the game trail that my deer and countless others followed. I trembled slightly as I looked closely at the worn path, imagined the deer, my deer, passing this way over and over again, looking for better forage, one eye cocked for intruders, one ear straining for the sound of a predator. Bending down a few yards off the road I opened my daypack and brought out the apples. Convinced I had placed them where my friend would find them I slowly retreated to the bright red machine that would whisk me away from here, would take me to a safer, more sheltered space.

Winter arrived at last in the valley, later than usual but making up for its tardiness with unusual vigor. Overnight the shrubs on the deck were powdered in frosty white, puddles from the last shower frozen solid. I thought of the high country and shivered. Soon there would be no grazing for months, the meadow grass buried under a blanket of snow, the leaves long gone from the trees. Nothing for a deer to eat unless it got very lucky. Or had a friend.

I approached the curve in the mountain road slowly, worried about ice on the pavement, nervous despite my being on four wheels this time, warmly ensconced within my aging Civic. The lack of snow surprised me, just a thin dusting on the frozen ground. The trail was, if anything, more clearly defined than before, the tall grass just off the shoulder beaten down a bit by wind and weather. As I emerged from the car I caught a glimpse of something, something brown, a few dozen feet from the road, barely visible in a shallow depression. My heart sank. I walked slowly toward it, watched its form emerge from the enclosing grass as I grew closer. It was a deer, dead, long dead in fact, laying on its right side, its body pointed away from the road, the far half of its carcass tangled in the long grass. Fallen as it tried to flee, wounded, hoping somehow to escape the fate brought upon it by some fast moving vehicle. I felt nauseous, light headed. I knew I should stop and catch my breath, maybe sit down for a moment, but I couldn't. I had to know.

I bent over the fallen animal and reached down to grasp its antler, the left one, the closest one. With as much strength as I could muster I both lifted and twisted, straining to turn the animal's head. I couldn't lift it, could not get the right side of the head separated from the grass. I realized why at once. The right antler was buried in the dirt, tangled in the grass. The right antler; this deer had both.

I stepped back and took a deep breath, my head spinning, my fingers tingling. I couldn't stop the tears, sat down and let them flow. After a while I stood up and looked around. Was it my imagination or was I being watched? Though I could see nothing in the meadow, still nothing among the trees, I couldn't shake the feeling. I turned slowly in place, my hand held high, blessing the four points of the compass. He was out there, I knew he was. I smiled. The crunching of the gravel as I walked back to the car was the most pleasant sound on the planet.

## *Dinner for One*

First the plate.

He places it carefully on the table, not too close to the edge. A thick plate, some sort of heavy ceramic, a soft orange brown. He recalls when he bought it, had to have it, the hue reminded him of the clay of Kenya, the color of the road that ran through his village, the rich deepness when it rained. Frowning, he rotates the plate slightly, turning it so the noticeable white chip on the edge is farthest from him, less obvious. He can almost pretend it isn't there.

Then the mug. He sets it above and slightly to the right, no more than two inches from the plate, close but not too close. He had wanted to put the wine glass there, the one from the set he and Chelsea were given on their wedding, the last of the four he had kept when they divorced. He had looked all over for it, only to realize it was in the storeroom, in the junk box along with a score of other broken utensils, implements, mementos awaiting repair. He was hard on glasses, she had always pointed that out to him, as if he didn't know, as if his clumsiness around delicate objects were some sudden discovery she was eager to share with him. So the mug is a stand-in, its stolid profile matching the bulk of the plate. It is a rich brown. Is that a good color in which to serve red wine? he asks himself. Yes, he thinks, yes, it will do quite nicely. Satisfied, he steps back and smiles.

Next the silverware. He snorts at the thought, *silverware*, as if the word demands an entire assemblage of metal objects rather than the single fork he first polishes on his shirttail. Silverware indeed! He is tempted to dispense with the artificiality of it all, just eat with his hands, the way he used to when he wanted to irritate Rachel. He chuckles at the thought, recalling her look of horror when her boss and his wife were over to dinner and he reached into the salad bowl to serve them. No, tonight he is feeling ceremonial – there will be a fork!

What is missing? He scowls, then realizes: a napkin. That will be easy. Not *too* easy; he won't be so crass as to rip a paper towel off the roll, not tonight. He disappears for a moment, returns triumphantly from the bedroom, a bandana in his hands. Not just any bandana, but the one he brought home from Nepal for Rachel, the one with the map of the Annapurna route carefully painted on. The one she thought she had lost when it came time to divide their belongings. He had kept quiet, knowing it was in his backpack, hoping she wouldn't remember.

Now the wine. An oaky, full-bodied cabernet, one he had been saving since Sara left him, a survivor of the tedious dissolution that left her with all the whites and pinot noirs. He smirks, remembering how her friends dismissed his taste, couldn't understand how she could be married to a clod who only liked wines he couldn't see through. Fuck 'em, he chuckles. His one regret is that they aren't here to see him drinking the bull's blood from his earthen chalice. He will try to remember to lift his pinky, just to show he has style.

All that is left is the meal itself. Not much to crow about, but it is his favorite, a thick slab of sockeye salmon, sparsely adorned with a bit of lemon, dill, black pepper, surely done by now, its rich aroma filling the small apartment. He hurries to the kitchen, returns with the sizzling portion balanced delicately on the blade of a too-small spatula, dropping it suddenly, with what will pass for a flourish, on the plate, juices splashing on the table, the bandana, his shirt. He ought to be upset with his clumsiness, he knows that, but tonight it doesn't matter. He has no intention of cleaning the grease stains, getting the dark smudges out of the surrogate napkin, off his sleeve. Tonight is all about living in the moment, he reminds himself. Don't sweat the small stuff.

At last he is ready. Looking around, taking in the dark room, the close boundaries of his current life, he is satisfied. This is good, he says aloud. This is very good. He pours the wine, takes a slow sip, letting the rich, dark fluid trickle over his tongue, tickle the back of his throat. Exhaling, he savors the vanilla and berry aromas. This is fabulous, he tells himself, the best wine I have ever had. Will ever have. He follows with a bite of the salmon, closes his eyes, embracing the sense of the sea that this fish, this rich, red-bodied fish, always evokes. He is happy; tears are trying to form at the edges of his eyes, his heart is racing slightly. Happy – that is how he wanted it, how he planned it, the only way that makes sense.

He reaches across the table to his right, to the empty place setting, the one that wasn't always empty, the one that more often than not served a laughing companion, a lover, a wife. Chelsea. Rachel. Sara. Amy. He smiles to think of them, of the lives intertwined, the rivers he has swum up, the bodies he has lost himself in, the mornings waking in a lover's arms.

It is time.

## *Blind Faith*

It was late Saturday morning, exactly one week before my high school commencement, when the kitchen phone rang. Mom and the younger kids were in the garden weeding and I had just come in from helping Dad string fence. I grabbed the phone eagerly, expecting it to be my girlfriend. We'd been a bit on the outs lately, and I was hoping to get back in her good graces.

To my disappointment the voice on the other end of the line belonged to my Uncle Woody. "Stevie, is that you?" he queried. Yes, I muttered, it was me. "I got your graduation present ready for you," he said. "You just have to meet me tomorrow morning at seven at the air park. Oh, and wear some good sturdy boots. And don't tell your mother." Having already strung together more words at one time than was his usual practice on the phone, Woody simply hung up – leaving me to ponder just what he had up his sleeve. With my uncle it seemed anything was possible.

Woody was a character. At least that's how my father described him. Other men who knew him chose less genteel terms: crazy-ass Okie and one wild SOB were among the other labels I had overhead. A little under six feet tall, barrel-chested with a square jaw, buzz cut, and no neck he looked every bit the veteran Navy flier he was. He wasn't really my uncle, but that was how I thought of him, how everyone in my family referred to him. He and his wife had taken a liking to me as an infant, and throughout my youth he carried a baby photo of me in his wallet. Of course I adored this big, gruff man. The same could not be said of my mother, who tolerated him largely because of his closeness to my father.

I suppose she had reason to be leery of Woody's interest in me. When I was twelve he let me take the stick of his small Aeronca, a vintage fabric-skinned tail dragger. When Mom found out it had been me at the controls when the little plane wing-wagged then buzzed our rural home she was livid. That was nothing, though, compared to her reaction when he gave me a subscription to Playboy for my sixteenth birthday. And then there was the time when he let me drive his car – without a license or even a learner's permit – some fifty miles home from a picnic because he was too drunk to get behind the wheel himself. Given the tension between the two I was quick to go along with Woody's request for secrecy.

Sunday morning found me pulling into the parking lot at the air park, only half awake, hoping whatever Woody had for me would be small, simple, and over with soon. I should have known better when I walked into the coffee shop and saw him sitting with Montana Bill, a fellow Navy veteran and one of the few men Woody would allow near his plane. As the two men huddled over their coffee in the booth nearest the door I couldn't help but notice what looked like a faded olive drab knapsack sitting on the bench next to them.

"Stevie, congratulations!" Woody bellowed as he embraced me in the customary bear hug. "You make me wish I'd finished school myself." Bill was his usual reserved self, mumbling something about college girls and what I had to look forward to on the East Coast. I had hoped to grab some breakfast but Woody was already pushing me out the door and angling toward the hangar where his weary old bird was parked. Bill trailed behind, holding the green pack. I began to feel a bit uneasy.

"It's like this, Stevie," Uncle Woody was saying as we entered the hangar. "Your mom and dad told me a while back that you were afraid of heights." Damn, I thought, how could they? Why would they expose my vulnerability to a man who made me feel inadequate just standing in the room with him? I felt the red flush rising in my cheeks as Woody went on. "So, I figured the best way to deal with a silly problem like that is to take the bull by the horns, spit in its eye, and grab the upper hand." I was overwhelmed, not just by the string of clichés he was spewing but by his unusual verbosity. Never a talker, he was being downright loquacious. Then, as he leaned in closer, I got a whiff of whiskey on his breath. Oh shit, I thought, this can't be good.

I helped Woody and Bill pull the small, light plane out onto the tarmac then stood waiting while they fiddled with their pre-flight rituals. About the time Bill walked over to me with the pack it dawned on me what was up. No, I told myself, that can't be a parachute. Woody wouldn't be that crazy. I could barely get myself to jump off the top of the barn into a pile of soft hay. What made him think I would jump out of a plane?

I took a closer look at the chute. It was old, a surplus item with USN stenciled on the side. Not the sort of thing that inspires trust, at least not in a teenage civilian. Woody saw me staring, picked up the chute, and took a step toward me. "It's no big deal, Stevie – actually it's a shitload of fun. Hell, I've jumped a couple of dozen times and was always ready to do it again. But hey, if you're scared to do it no problem – we can just go up for a nice fly, cruise around the valley. Something safe."

That did it. I may have been terrified at heart but I was not going to appear a coward in Woody's eyes. "So how does this thing work?" I found myself asking.

As we circled slowly upward, Woody gave me the scoop. It was simple, really. All I had to do was slip out the door when he cut the prop, push out and down, count to ten, and pull the ripcord. Easy, he said. Meanwhile I was doing my best not to hyperventilate. I was scared out of my mind, nearly paralyzed with fright, but too stubborn and self-conscious to back down. "Is that a slow ten or a fast ten?" I queried. "It's whatever ten you want" was his chuckling reply.

I pondered that for a moment. "Couldn't we use a static line instead? Should I really be doing this on my first jump?"

"Nah," he explained, his whiskey breath wafting over to me, "there's no fun in that. Trust me, you'll be fine. I fitted the pilot chute and the cord to this rig myself. Done it before a bunch of times. No way it's not gonna work. You'll do just fine."

At last we were at the desired altitude, which was higher than I had anticipated. Woody pointed out my landing site, a mercifully large pasture surrounded by a wide expanse of low crops – and an absence of trees, thank God. "There's no wind to speak of, it oughta be a cinch," he said, "You can pull on the chute cords a little if you have to. It ain't really steering but you'll get the hang of it." I felt the fear viscerally now, a tight clenching starting in my chest and working its way down to my groin. I worried I was going to pee my pants. Woody cut the engine and the plane drifted quietly for a few seconds. The wind whooshing over the wings was the loudest sound on the planet. Oddly, I felt the fierce grip of fear loosen a bit. I concentrated on a reassuring bit of probability, mind over matter. Lots of people jump out of airplanes, I told myself, some over and over again. It can't be that risky, can it? I undid my seat harness, crouched half-upright, and moved in a fog of self-deception to meet my fate.

On Woody's signal I opened the door, turned my back so I faced outward, grabbed with both hands like he had instructed, and tried not to look down as I slipped out and away. I almost made a clean break, I came oh so close to just dropping smoothly like a rock, eyes glued to the horizon. At the last second my elbow caught the strut ever so slightly, just enough to twist me around. I found myself falling half backward, half sideways, skewed in an ungainly posture, now plummeting somewhere between head first and upside down, feeling like a turtle turned on its back. It was hard catching my breath as the wind whistled by, all I could do to slowly, laboriously rotate my body, try to get myself untwisted. It took forever, but finally I was squared away, my body canted forward, more or less upright. Then I looked down.

The ground seemed much, much closer to me than when I'd first looked out the door of the Aeronca. I started counting – one, a thousand, two, a thousand, three… I never made it to four. I realized with a sick shudder that I had no idea how long I'd been dropping before I began my tally, was terrified I'd already used up my allotted number of seconds, and then some. I grabbed frantically for the ripcord.

It wasn't there.

Panic, tired of lurking in the wings, pushed simple fright aside. I could hear my heartbeat pounding explosively, felt the slick oiliness of fear wash over my body. I was going to die. I had to force myself to think logically, to analyze the situation, not let my brain shut down in terror. I knew the cord had been there earlier, it couldn't have just gone away. Let me think, what might have happened? Then I realized – in my twisting and turning it must have gotten pushed around, had migrated somehow. I began to search for it, running my hand in an ever-widening circle around the spot where I knew the cord had once been. At first nothing, then – Eureka! As soon as my fingers closed on the comfortable, familiar strand my heart slowed. I felt strangely calm, as if nothing mattered anymore, as if finding the cord was all that was required. I was safe.

Well… perhaps not yet. There was still the problem of the ground growing steadily nearer. I could see details in the field below with frightening clarity and precision. I recalled Woody's instructions, pulled quickly and firmly out and down on the cord. Nothing happened; an awful second or two passed. Then, with a jolt that threatened to jerk me out of the harness, the big round chute opened. Relief washed over me, I was close to tears. I looked up and felt for all the world as if I were trapped in the tentacles of a huge jellyfish. Looking down again I was relieved; the ground was approaching at a much more leisurely rate than before. I started laughing, partly because my underwear was still dry, but mostly because I knew I would make it out of this insane episode alive. The buoyant feeling, suspended in midair by this contraption of ancient cloth, was exhilarating. I watched the grassy field get closer, closer, then… wham! I hit the ground like a rock dropped on concrete, my knees felt like they'd been driven up past my armpits. The chute settled gently over the top of me, a soft gossamer lid shutting out the sky. I lay on the ground several seconds, making sure nothing was broken, thankful to be done with the ordeal, thankful to be alive.

I'd been sitting on the warm grass for what seemed like hours when I finally caught a glimpse of Woody's beat up pickup turning off the road, watched it bouncing along the uneven ground toward me. As he pulled up and got out of the cab I looked past him, noticed another vehicle entering the pasture. This one was black and white and had a flashing red light atop its roof. I smiled; not for the first time had Woody aroused the ire of some less-than-understanding citizen. Jumping without proper clearance into a stranger's pasture was perhaps not the most legal thing to do.

Woody was all grin as he walked up to me, simultaneously patting me on the back while hugging the breath out of me. He was as exuberant as I'd ever seen him. "How about that, Stevie? Wasn't that more fun than a week in a whorehouse? Didn't I tell you you'd do just fine?" I tried to match his enthusiasm but was feeling way too exhausted to be that celebratory. "Yeah, it was pretty cool" was all I could muster by way of reply. "That's it? Just pretty cool?" He looked a bit dejected at my answer; I felt guilty immediately. "No, Uncle Woody, it was more than that. It was fantastic. I even kinda liked the free fall part of it," I lied. He looked over his shoulder at the police cruiser that had just pulled up abreast of his GMC, then back at me. "Really?" he asked. Yes, I assured him, really – it was an amazing experience. "Okay then, I've got just one question," he said, a mischievous grin spreading across his rough features.

"Why did you pull the cord after only five seconds?

# *Merrick of Batua*

Robert Merrick was nursing his fourth or fifth pint of Tusker at the poolside bar of the Jacaranda Hotel when he became aware of an animated discussion a few tables away. A slightly plump American tourist in shorts and a low-cut sleeveless top was angrily berating a young Kenyan man, who was maintaining an uncomfortable smile throughout her tirade.

Focusing as best he could through the encroaching alcoholic fog, Merrick soon made out the situation; the stoic Kikuyu was her personal tour guide. It seemed the woman had wanted to see Kenyans, *real* Kenyans, not the besuited members of the business class seated around thc bar nor the carefully made-up "traditional dancers" her guide had shown her that afternoon at the Bomas of Kenya. Where were the *real* Kenyans, the traditional warriors? she demanded. She had paid good money and endured an infinitely long plane ride, and dammit she wanted to see authentic tribesmen! She had had her fill of waiters, minivan drivers, and leering young men in polyester bell-bottoms and ragged T-shirts. She couldn't care less about animals – there was a zoo back home – but colorful natives were another matter.

She'd been in the country two days already and was losing her patience.

With great effort, and what passed for good balance, Merrick made his way over to her table. "*Shauri gani?*" he asked the woman's bedeviled companion. The man shrugged, with the slightest rolling of his eyes, a gesture not lost on the now sullen American. "My name is Robert," Merrick said, turning his attention to her. "May I buy you a beer and try to straighten out this matter for you?" Her relieved smile said yes.

Several drinks later, he had her in his thrall. "Never mind the Maasai," he was telling her. "They're hopelessly corrupted, modernized, poor imitations of their grandfathers. Not worth wasting your time on. Why, they even send their children to school! Now *my* tribe, the Samburu, they're different." He felt a wee bit of guilt at this, as he thought of his own students and how he'd had to persuade several parents to allow their children to continue despite poor marks and the high cost of school fees. "The people of my village would die before they would wear modern dress." Unless, of course, one counted his cast off T-shirts, the jeans that made their way up from the market in Maralal, and the wool jacket he gave away once he realized he'd never need it in Batua. "They know what it means to keep tradition alive. Let me tell you about the Samburu circumcision rituals..."

Merrick woke to the sound of soft snoring beside him and the dull pounding of a killer hangover in his head.

Stumbling into the bathroom to take a leak (God, how he loved indoor plumbing! So much nicer than squatting over a hole, looking out for scorpions), he tried to replay the events of the prior evening. Not much to recall, except a vague memory of soft white flesh and small sharp teeth. Must have been great, he told himself. Wish I'd been there. To his relief, he was able to slink woozily back to the side of the bed, dress more or less quickly, and slip out without waking... what was her name? Terry? Tammy? Traci?... yeah, that was it. Traci.

***

Merrick had nearly let the Peace Corps pass him by. As his college years drew to an end he distanced himself from idealistic classmates swayed by the exhortations of a dead president. They went off to live in sweltering bamboo huts in Thailand or to teach Nepalese the finer points of chicken rearing; he stayed behind to wallow in a post-commencement malaise. A sheltered West Coast boy, it had been all he could manage to adapt to life in urban New England. Teaching English in Papua New Guinea or helping villagers rear tilapia in muddy ponds in Ghana was out of the question.

It was not until he found himself in graduate school, with a thesis advisor who had been a Volunteer in East Africa, that Merrick began to give the Peace Corps a second thought. One day after classes, downing beers together in a dingy campus pub, he was intrigued by many of the man's revelations about the Dark Continent. Merrick had grown up assuming that all of Africa was inhospitable, a muggy mélange of jungle and swamp, a nether region filled with disease and ritualistic murderers who preyed on hapless white travelers. To learn that parts of Africa had a pleasant climate, friendly people, and a near absence of contagion was intriguing. Perhaps, he thought, there was some distant place – at least in Africa – where he could indulge his philanthropic impulses without expiring in the process. Maybe it was possible to be altruistic and adventurous without paying too high a price. Perhaps... perhaps someday he'd have the balls to actually set foot in a developing country. Meanwhile he had a thesis to write and a long-suffering wife impatient for him to get his butt into the labor force. He knew full well she had no interest in moving to any place without running water.

Two years after his divorce Merrick was lying on a sand dune in Death Valley, contemplating his uncertain future with a head full of marijuana, when his new lover suggested he join the Peace Corps. Sure, he thought, why not. Merrick dusted off an old image of himself in Albert Schweitzer regalia, doing enlightened good works in some tropical backwater. Then he got to thinking about his advanced age. Wasn't the Peace Corps for idealistic young fools fresh out of college? All his friends had joined in their early twenties. Surely the Corps wouldn't want a cynical old fart of thirty-three.

It turned out they did.

***

Merrick's excitement at being placed in East Africa, his clear first choice when he'd filled out the application, began to fade as soon as he set foot on the continent. Peace Corps training was a miserable experience, and he couldn't wait for it to end. The daily tedium of lesson planning, practice teaching, and Swahili language instruction wore on him. He found his Kenyan practice students too amiable, his in-country trainers oddly mellow and a bit condescending. He hated the food, the beer was vile and, except for a ghastly concoction made from papayas, the wine was nonexistent. He was sick for several weeks following his arrival, and lay for hours on the cold cement floor of the dormitory wondering why he'd come to such a cold, rainy, decidedly non-tropical part of Africa. It was arguably the longest three months of his life. He struggled to keep his spirits up, told himself repeatedly that he might still come to enjoy Peace Corps life – if he could just survive the prelude.

Several days before the end of training the new Volunteers were given their assignments. With minimal ceremony a list was posted in the dining hall. There were cries of delight and frantic comparing of sites. Some got the Coast, and were already planning to visit their friends in the highlands en route to Mt. Kenya, while others from the highlands wondered how easily they could slip into Nairobi on weekends without being caught by the Peace Corps brass. Two Volunteers, a man and woman who could barely tolerate the sight of each other, found themselves posted to the same school. Another Volunteer was to be placed in Nairobi, yet another in Kisumu.

Merrick quickly found his name, then the name of his school: Batua Harambee Secondary. He'd never heard of Batua, even though he had spent hours poring over a detailed map of the country planning two years of vacations. To make matters worse, none of the Kenyan training staff had a clue to its whereabouts either. One language trainer thought it might be near the Tanzanian border, but he wasn't sure. Another said he had heard of a village with a similar name near Malindi. Merrick began to have a sinking feeling. After much inquiry, an elderly cook who claimed to know of Batua was summoned from the kitchen. When told that the American was to be a teacher there, the old man began giggling mischievously. "The *mwalimu* should drink very much now," he chortled, "for he will not be finding the water in Batua".

***

To call Batua a village required considerable imagination. Strewn along a dirt track heading north in the general direction of Loiangalanyi, standing apart from the scores of small thatched huts that blanketed the area, were four seemingly identical mud walled buildings. Their roofs were of *mabati*, corrugated steel that rusted at the mere contemplation of rain and served to hold the day's intense heat long after the sun had set. Upon closer inspection, one building stood out as the local bar, another as a *duka*, or general store. The role of the remaining two was less clear. The westernmost one gave no clue to its function – hardly surprising since it had been vacant for more than a year. A former tea shop, its owner had forsaken the acacia scrub for the bright lights, paved streets, and predictable beer supply of Nairobi. The remaining edifice, only slightly larger than the others and featuring a few more glassless windows, was the local school. It was there that Robert Merrick was assigned to spend the better part of two years performing what was frequently – and sarcastically – referred to as the toughest job he'd ever love.

It really wasn't that bad. After a rough first month, Merrick had accumulated an impressive array of water containers – jerry cans, old cooking oil containers, and an empty Scotch bottle from the Catholic mission in Maralal. These he kept as full as possible, lined up against the wall of his mud and wattle hut. It wasn't true there was no water. There was damned little water, and you had to work your butt off or pay dearly for it, but it was there. He soon hired a second form student who needed school fees to trudge the several kilometers to the nearest water source, a salty seasonal stream that trickled all but a month or two of the year. When that source dried up, there were a few wells farther to the North, but of course the water from there was even more costly. It seemed most of Merrick's spare shillings went for water. Or beer. It quickly became clear to him that, at the peak of the dry season, it was cheaper and safer to drink the foul product of Kenya Breweries, Ltd than the murky, sulfurous liquid alternative. Bathing and laundry were a problem, of course, but only for him. The rest of the village exhibited remarkable economy when it came to using water for personal hygiene. After a while, Merrick found he could get along just fine with a weekly sponge bath, and a pair of underwear could go for nearly as long if one remembered to turn them inside-out from time to time.

Food was plentiful, so long as you didn't mind dried beans, dried maize, and the occasional leathery bit of goat. Merrick quickly developed a taste for soured milk, which kept for weeks with no refrigeration in a calabash hanging from the wall above his precious water vessels.

To his surprise and delight the teaching was fun. His school was the only one in a radius of perhaps thirty kilometers, so he had quite a number of students from other villages living with relatives and family friends in Batua in order to attend. Even so, his classes were small – first form was fourteen in number, while he had only five in fourth form. Their ages ranged from thirteen to twenty-two, and all were frighteningly intent on learning. Despite the lack of textbooks and other amenities deemed essential back home, his students would always have their homework done on time, would copy his blackboard scrawls with great accuracy in their thin exercise books. Respectful, well-mannered, hard working – they were not at all what he expected high school students to be. He felt lucky indeed.

Taking stock of the situation after his first year in the village, Merrick was astonished at how content he was. Most all the Volunteers, himself included, had assumed he would be the first of the group to terminate early. Instead he seemed to thrive in the harsh aesthetic of his new existence. He was even thinking of extending his service for a third year.

***

It was a typically hot Batua afternoon. Lunch was finished, and Merrick was trying to interest his third form students in the finer points of quadratic equations. He was about to write the damned formula on the board one more time when he noticed that most of his students weren't looking at him. They were staring out the window with rapt attention. He was about to say something when half the class – those seated farthest from the window – suddenly rushed across the room to share the view. Holding back his anger, Merrick calmly walked to the door and stepped outside to see what the fuss was about. There, in the dirt courtyard by the flag, holding on to the headmaster's arm as she squinted toward him in the bright sun, was Traci.

Panic fought with nausea for control of Merrick's emotions, and both declared a draw.

"What the ... How did you... ?"

"You could at least say you're happy to see me," Traci sniffed. "God knows it was a pain in the ass tracking you down. The bitch at the Peace Corps Office wouldn't give me a bit of information on how to find you and nobody at my hotel had even heard of Batua! If I hadn't bumped into your friend Shawn I wouldn't have made it here. Thank God he took me to the station and got me on the right bus; there is no way I'd have gone to that part of Nairobi on my own. Where do all those beggars come from, anyway? Somebody should be doing something to help those poor people. It was so depressing. Do you have any idea what my trip was like? Oh hell, of course you do. I just don't know how you stand it. If I had to spend all day breathing diesel fumes, crammed into broken down buses and then those wretched *matatu*s full of goats and puking babies, just to go two hundred miles I don't think I'd *ever* leave my village!"

Merrick was still floating in a sea of apprehension, only half-listening to her tirade. The other half of his attention was divided between frantically considering and rejecting ways out of his current predicament and contemplating what cruel violence he would personally inflict on his buddy Shawn the next time he encountered that big-mouthed sack of shit. This has to be a bad dream, he tried to tell himself, *just the effects of my anti-malarial meds*, but he knew full well he had himself and not the chloroquine to blame.

It gradually dawned on Merrick that Traci had finished her rant some time ago, and both she and the headmaster were looking at him expectantly. Glancing around the compound one last time for an escape route, and finding none, he steeled himself to the reality confronting him. "Traci, of course I'm delighted to see you again. I just wasn't expecting it, that's all. How long are you planning to stay? I'll need to ask around and find a place –"

"Hold it right there! I clearly remember you saying that if I made it up to Batua you'd be happy to put me up, show me around, give me an experience to remember. Why the hell do you think I'm here? I want to see the real Africa, and you promised you'd show it to me."

Her last line was delivered with a pout bordering on tearful, and Merrick felt he had lost all control of the situation. *Oh well*, he thought, *it could be worse*. It looked like he'd be having a roommate for a few days, a week at the most. It shouldn't take much longer than that before the appeal of life in a drought-stricken village with no modern amenities lost its charm and Traci returned to Nairobi. At least in the future he'd be more careful what he promised strange women when he tried to get them in the sack.

It was then that Merrick became aware of Daoudi, the headmaster, still standing quietly off to his side, of his students staring with silent intensity from the classroom windows, of the other staff members who had come out of the school office to witness the odd reunion of these two Americans. Oh shit, he thought, now what.

It was Daoudi, a fellow bachelor and frequent drinking partner of Merrick's, who broke the expectant silence. "It is good that your friend has come, Mr. Robert. You must be very happy! I will be welcome to take your classes this afternoon so you can properly greet your visitor." Then, his eyes fixed on Traci's ample bosom, Daoudi added, “Perhaps I can join you and your friend for dinner this evening?”

Merrick groaned his acceptance, turned, and walked off toward home while a pair of skinny Form I students burst from the closest classroom and fought for the privilege of carrying Traci's heavy backpack.

***

Life in Batua changed dramatically in just a few days. Traci's demanding nature showed no signs of mellowing. Where before Merrick would carry home an armful of exercise books most every night, he now had no time to correct even the simplest algebra problems, was unable to read a single short composition. His new companion sucked all his energy. Time that should have been devoted to lesson planning was spent taking Traci around the village to meet people he himself didn't know. Evenings were spent in bed – not a bad way to spend them, mind you, but not at all what he needed to be effective in the classroom. He felt he was falling hopelessly behind, that he was failing his students.

At least, he had hoped, she would be happy to be in a village with real live Samburu, even if only a few still wore blankets. That hope faded quickly. “Shoes” she said with scorn the second day.

“Shoes?” he replied.

“Yeah, cheesy damned Western shoes – just like the ones you can get at any Payless. I thought your Samburu would be barefoot, or at most wearing sandals made of buffalo hide or something. Doesn't strike me as terribly traditional."

It wasn't long before Merrick came to dread coming home to his small hut. Despite urging his guest to go out and mingle with the locals on her own, she seemed reluctant to do anything without him at her side. All morning and into the afternoon she would stay close to home, venturing no more than a few huts' distance from his, struggling to find something to talk about with the *mamas* and curious *watoto* who were his immediate neighbors. The moment Merrick walked through the door Traci would give vent to her cabin fever, would demand that they do something together. Or, to be more accurate, that *he* do something to entertain her. He was wearing out the few friendships he had made in Batua trying to include her in the rich social life she imagined he led. Despite his coaching her on proper dress and behavior in a somewhat traditional rural community, Traci continued to expose her shoulders and legs, and could not comprehend why she was rarely offered a beer when her hosts presented Merrick with one. When he tried to explain that, in these parts, only prostitutes dressed and acted as she did, Traci was completely unsympathetic. She was not, she insisted, an African and there was no way anyone could expect her to abide by such silly rules. Least of all him. Okay, Merrick thought, I won't push the issue. Given her reluctance to explore on her own, he was pretty sure he could keep her away from embarrassing situations.

By the afternoon of Traci's seventh day in Batua he had reached a breaking point. He just couldn't go straight home after school; he desperately needed some calm time without his chatty constant companion. After classes had ended he made his decision, and turned left rather than right as he departed the building. Soon he had found his way quietly to the nearly empty bar. There, in the dim light cast by the one small window, he ordered a Tusker and settled in to ponder his current fate.

Within a few minutes Njuguna, a fellow teacher, had drifted in; he was followed shortly by Barsolai, the school's bursar. Soon empty bottles were crowding the small table as the men expounded passionately on the usual topics: women, football, and politics. A couple of locals joined them and were quick to add their voices to the increasingly animated discussion.

In the midst of making what he felt was an important point about the goalkeeper for the Harambee Stars, Merrick suddenly noticed he was the only one talking. All eyes were on the door. It took a second or two for it to register, but the silhouette poised in the bright doorway of this solidly male bastion was feminine. And it was clearly not wearing a skirt. His heart sunk.

Once her eyes had adjusted to the gloom, Traci stormed over to his table. "Just what the hell do you think you're doing leaving me home while you go off drinking with your buddies?" she snarled. "I was *so* bored I could hardly stand it. I'm sorry but there is only so much talk about children, chickens, and drunken husbands I can endure. Your neighbors are the dullest people on the face of the planet. And why didn't you tell me there was a bar in this place? At least I could have been killing time here rather that reading your stupid *Newsweeks* for the umpteenth time. I could kill for a cold beer about now."

She sat down abruptly and crossed her arms with an angry harrumph. Then, with every pair of eyes in the room glued to her, she crossed her legs as well. The silence was deafening, the leers from the patrons impossible even for her to ignore. "What?" she whispered to Merrick. "Is it something I said? Why are all those lechers staring at me?"

Merrick hid his head in his hands, closed his eyes, and wished he were anywhere but here.

By the next morning Traci had consented to dress more conservatively. Merrick found a shirt of his with sleeves that fit her reasonable well. He came back from a visit to Eunice, the school clerk, with a *kanga* Traci could wear as a wrap around skirt. Modeling her new outfit for him, he allowed a sigh of relief. Though with her glowing white skin she would never fit in, at least she would not draw so much attention to herself everywhere she went.

Merrick was also relieved when Traci announced she was going to go out exploring during the day while he was at work. *Wonderful*, he thought, *maybe she'll gain a bit of independence, won't be so damned needy of me whenever we're together*.

A few days later, as he was sipping on a warm Tusker, unwinding from another day of prepping his fourth form students for their exit exams, Traci burst happily into the hut. "I've been invited – we've been invited to dinner! And she's the coolest old lady, I love her, she's the color of ebony, she has these amazing stretched ear lobes with some incredible earrings. And her necklace… it's made of ostrich shell with these weird little bones – no, wait, I think they're teeth – sticking out. I told her we could come tonight, I was sure you'd want to come with me. She says she knows you. Her name is Nasawa. I'm so excited, I think she wants to be my friend! So, can we go?"

Merrick groaned quietly. He had never heard the name before, most likely had never met the old mama. Of course she knew him. Everyone in and around Batua knew him, he stood out like a kernel of maize in a cow pie. The thought of spending the evening in a smoky hut making small talk in *Kiswahili* depressed him. Still, Traci had shown some initiative. He couldn't bring himself to throw cold water on her first efforts. "Sure," he said, "just give me a few more minutes to relax. Then I'll swing by the *duka* for a packet of *chai* and some sugar."

"Huh?" grunted Traci, "Why do you need to do that now? Don't we have enough already?"

"It's not for us," he replied. "If we're sharing a meal with Nasawa we need to bring a gift. It would appear selfish if we showed up empty handed. People would talk."

When they arrived at Nasawa's compound, a few kilometers from the school in a direction he rarely strolled, Merrick's heart sunk. This was to be no simple meal, rather it had grown into a major social event. At least a dozen young Samburu men were loitering outside the compound while another five or six flanked the door to Nasawa's hut. A few young women held timidly back. Dinner was already being prepared. *Sufurias* of water had been put on the fire, soon to be filled with *ugali*. From somewhere close by came sounds of chopping. A large pot of *busaa* – traditional beer with all the characteristics of runny vomit – was being carried in by two young girls, struggling to keep from spilling any of the odorous contents. A small boy followed in their footsteps. Merrick smiled when he saw the little one furtively sneak his fingers into the pot and lick them clean.

Then he saw the goat.

It was rather plump for a local creature, probably someone's favorite. Its sad brown eyes caught Merrick's as it was led into the compound and he had to turn away. Damn – why couldn't Nasawa have served them a *kuku* or two? Rubber chicken he could tolerate, but he could barely abide *nyama choma* . Oh well, he thought, at least it's traditional cooking – Traci should be pleased.

Chairs were produced for the guests and bottles of Tusker were brought out from the relative cool of the maize shed – it appeared they would be spared the *busaa*, another sign of the importance of their visit. Nasawa, together with a young woman who was probably her daughter, pulled their chairs up across from the *mwalimu* and his companion, and stared at them expectantly. Merrick solemnly presented the *chai* and *sukari*, which was accepted with a polite "*asante*".

Immediately the crowd of young men closed in around them, all asking questions at once. Nasawa beamed, basking in the importance of the occasion. "Showtime," Merrick muttered under his breath as he prepared to spend the next hour answering questions about himself, his lady friend, America, and the entire white race – all the while translating from *Kiswahili* for Traci's benefit. He felt a headache coming on.

Suddenly Traci gripped his arm. He felt her shudder, turned to see what was upsetting her so. A few meters away, not quite hidden from view by Nasawa's hut, a grinning youth was dispatching the unfortunate goat. With a dull knife, no less, sawing laboriously to cut through its wiry neck. The goat bleated pathetically, then fell quiet. Traci was transfixed, mortified. She hardly drew a breath the entire time the poor animal was being gutted, skinned, and quartered. Her nails dug deeper into Merrick's arm with each cut of the *panga*. Meanwhile he did his best to entertain queries from the audience, trying to keep his sidelong glances at Traci's stricken face to a minimum. Only when what remained of the goat had been whisked away did she loosen her grasp.

After what seemed an eternity, a young woman appeared at their side with a basin of water with which to rinse their hands. Food was brought to them on steaming plates. Nasawa had spared no expense – besides the usual mound of *ugali* there was both cabbage and *sukuma wiki* and a few small hot *pili pili* to spice the meal. And goat. Each of the honored guests had several chunks of barely cooked meat, along with a piece or two of innards, crowded on their plates. Traci looked at hers with a horrified expression, started shaking, and stood up quickly sending the plate and its contents flying. "I can't," she sobbed, "I just can't... I'm sorry!" She turned, her eyes wide, her arms jerking, and sprinted out of the compound, leaving Merrick behind. Nasawa was aghast, half the young men were yelling angrily, the rest laughing and rolling their eyes.

Merrick shook his head, sighed, and tried to explain what had happened to his host. Sadly, he could not find the right words in *Kiswahili*. Perhaps it was just as well.

***

Within a few days Traci had settled back into her routine. The episode with the goat, if not forgotten, was at least overcome. And still, despite her continued complaints about Batua – its corrupted culture, the absence of comforts, the boredom she felt so acutely – Traci made no attempt at leaving. It seemed to Merrick that she was perversely content to remain in the village, that she had somehow lost sight of what it was she had come there for. As she neared the end of her second week's stay it began to look like she might be settling in. The thought of this loud, insensitive woman being his long-term companion threatened to sink Merrick into his first spell of serious depression since coming to this harsh land.

Casting about for a way out of his predicament, he came up with a plan. Not a good plan by any means, but at least it offered a glimmer of hope. The Turkana Bus might well be his salvation. An aging overland lorry, it carried a dozen or so backpacking tourists, hearty souls searching for something beyond the typical cushy game park experience, north from the capital to the shore of Lake Turkana. The Bus took the main road, passing through a small village several kilometers from Batua at least once a month. He was friends with the drivers; they gave him lifts to or from Nairobi now and again. If – and it was a *big* if – he could get Traci on the bus she would get to see more of her precious "real" Kenyans than the shoe-clad Samburu loitering about Batua. The Turkana were the real deal – badass, half-naked warriors the color of ebony, who rubbed animal fat on their bodies to keep their skin from cracking under the harsh desert sun. Even their women were hard and fierce enough to scare the bejeesus out of most Westerners who encountered them. They should be more than traditional enough for Traci. Perhaps then, having seen her fill of what she came for, she could be convinced to return to Nairobi and let him get on with his life.

The best-laid plans have a way of disintegrating. Merrick intended to broach the subject of the Turkana Bus that night, Traci's twelfth in the village. He thought sometime after dinner, but before their nightly roll in the hay, would be the right time. And it probably would have been – had she been there for dinner. At the end of the school day Merrick arrived home to an empty hut. No problem, he thought, she's out visiting with one of the mamas or watching the goats being milked. He had a couple of shots of cheap Indian whiskey and a secretive puff on a joint while waiting. Still no Traci. He fixed dinner, expecting her to walk through the door at any moment. Rather than let the *ugali* and *sukuma* get cold, he ate supper without her. What little concern he felt for Traci's absence slipped away with another shot or two. She's a big girl, he said to himself as he drifted off to sleep, I'm sure she can find her way back on her own.

The next morning Merrick awoke in a mild panic. The other half of the bed was still empty, there was no sign of Traci having been in the hut at all during the night. Surprised at the anxious feelings taking hold of him, he took a deep breath and tried to think things through. Surely she was still in the village – there was no chance she'd have ventured into the bush where hyenas or God knows what other dangers lurked. Forcing himself to remain calm he got quickly dressed and set off to Daoudi's house.

After Merrick had called out *hodi* twice, the door to the headmaster's house slowly opened. His friend came sheepishly out, clad only in a pair of trousers. "Mr. Robert, what causes you to be seeing me so early in the morning? Is there a problem?" He was about to share his worry over Traci's absence when he caught a brief glimpse of blond hair and pale skin inside, moving quickly past the open door. Relief, anger, and jealousy wrestled for control of his emotions. Anger won. He spun on his heel and, without saying a word, stormed back to his hut.

Merrick drifted through his day on automatic pilot, going through the motions of teaching with his mind far from the task at hand. He debated with himself the merits of simply ignoring Traci's defection versus laying claim to the woman who had – surprisingly – gotten somehow under his skin. He was of both minds, torn in each direction, unable to make a decision. He drifted home, long after classes had ended, in a robotic trance.

No sooner did he have the charcoal lighted in his *jiko* than he heard an unmistakable sound. An automobile had pulled into the school compound, and a large one at that. As the dust stirred up by the vehicle drifted past his hut he heard a voice – an American, clearly not a Kenyan – calling his name. Curious and a bit alarmed, he rushed out the door, nearly colliding with a tall blond man with pale skin and clothes too clean and new for this part of the country. He recognized Dave Morgan at once. The man responsible for all of Northern Kenya, Dave rarely left the Nairobi office, preferring to deal by mail – if at all – with the handful of Volunteers that were his charge. Something was clearly up. Merrick's first thought was of the bong he had in plain sight on his bedside table, his first emotion fear of being caught in this flagrant violation of Peace Corps policy.

He needn't have worried, Dave had graver concerns. "Pack your bag, grab what you need, we leave here in ten minutes!" he barked.

*What the hell*, thought Merrick, *where's the fire?* Then he noticed Amber Dowd, his nearest Peace Corps neighbor, a rural health Volunteer from a village several hours away, sitting uncomfortably in the back seat of the Land Rover. Her eyes were red, her expression downcast. Damn! "What's up," he stammered, "what's going on?"

"No time to explain the details," Morgan shouted back, "just get your shit together and let's go. There's been a coup. We can't guarantee how long Kenyatta Airport will stay open. The Army is in control and they say we have safe passage, but you never know…"

Numb, Merrick dragged his dusty duffel from under the bed and tried to think of what to fill it with. Sensing his disorientation, Morgan began grabbing books off shelves, clothing from the neat pile on the floor, even the resinous pipe from beside the bed and started stuffing them into the bag. When most of his meager possessions had been packed, Morgan turned to him and sighed. "Okay, I can give you a minute or two to tidy things up. Just make it quick. Anybody here you need to say goodbye to?".

Robert Merrick looked around dazedly, at the school building empty of students at this late hour, at the village that had been his home for the past year, the red dirt soccer field, Daoudi's house. His gaze lingered on the home of his friend and teaching mate. He was overcome by a poignant sensation, an odd mix of regret and relief. A smile slowly crossed his face.

"No," he said, "No – I don't need to say goodbye to anyone."

"Let's just go."

## *Jack*

Hi there, how ‘ya doin, my name’s Jack. And yours is? Okay Al, good to meet you! So you’re headed to Galveston too, eh? First time on this airline? Well, let me tell you, this wasn’t *my* first choice, nosiree. Not after working on these ancient 727s in Uganda. Yeah, that’s right, East Africa. No, Idi Amin has been long gone, Obote too, the murderous bastard. Worse than Amin by a long shot. Got a new guy in there now, Museveni, started out good but lately he’s been getting as power crazy as the rest of ‘em.

Where was I going with this? Oh yeah, that’s right, 727s. We used them a lot in the Company, decent low altitude aircraft, for a jet anyway. I know, you’re thinking that’s *way* too big a bird to put down on some half-mile runway in the middle of Bumfuck, Nowhere. Well, lemme tell you, Al, our drivers could drop those puppies into places you wouldn’t believe, end up with their nose so deep in the jungle they had to hack their way out the door. And takeoffs? Hell, it was like riding an elevator! So yeah, a little bigger than I would have liked but when you gotta get a few dozen of your guys in and out in a hurry they did the trick.

Which company? Nah, you got it wrong. I'm talking about THE Company, Al. You know, CIA. Black ops stuff, secret shit. The sort of stuff your average Joe doesn't read about in the paper. What did I do? Well, if I told you I'd have to kill you. Heh heh, just jokin' there Al, don't go getting all jumpy on me now.

So anyways, back to these airplanes, like the crates we're riding in now. We were kinda stuck with them out in the field, sorta standard issue if you catch my drift. I got no gripe with old technology, hell we'd still be flying C47s in and out of shitholes if they were fast enough to outrun cheapass third world fighters. Not that the Seven Two Seven is any speed demon, not in the least. But where we fly 'em, way out in the bush, never too far from a border, they're fast enough. Only lost three or four of them that I know of, one in Uganda – that was engine failure – a couple in the CAR. The CAR? Oh, hell, sorry – Central African Republic, pissant little country, couldn't find a decent beer there if your life depended on it. Oh yeah, and one in Chad. Guess that one wasn't quite fast enough. Our own fault, I suppose – never should have sold those old F5s to the government there, though none of us thought their pilots would ever figure out how to fly the damned things. Guess we underestimated the African mind, eh?

Hang on a minute. Miss? Yeah, thanks, can you get me another Johnny Walker and – what's that you're drinking Al? White wine? No shit, you're a wine drinker? Sorry, don't mean to sound rude. Yeah, Miss, bring another white wine for my friend Al here. Hell, make both of 'em doubles, we gotta screw up our courage if we're gonna keep riding in one of these jalopies.

So anyway, Al, back to the 727s. Did you know what pieces of shit the engines are on these things? I mean, under normal circumstances they're fine, no problem, just keep ticking. But throw in a few good sized birds, or even a fair to middling flock of little ones, and it's no fun at all. The one we lost in Uganda tried to eat a Marabou stork – ever seen one of them? Goddam, they have to be the ugliest bird in all creation, big things, look like a cross between a heron and a pelican, with a little turkey thrown in for good measure. Clogged up the engine real good just as the plane was taking off. Plowed into a baobab at the end of the runway, nothing left after the fire but a black smudge. Oh well, shit happens.

Ever been to Galveston before, Al? No? Well, it's not a bad city, a little dirty is all, smells a bit like shrimp but that's just the Gulf gets in your nose. Plenty to do there. What's that? Are there many birds there? Hell yes, there's tons of them, most any kind of bird you can imagine. You're a bird watcher? Really – a white wine drinking bird watcher? Well, I'll be damned. You'll like the pelicans then, lots of them around Galveston, especially over the water out near the airport. What? Oh hell, don't go getting' all worried on me, I'm sure there's no real danger. Still… you did pay attention when the stewardess was talking about flotation cushions, right? Good, good, you'll do just fine if anything happens. Not that anything's gonna happen, just pays to be prepared. It can't hurt.

Say, do you smell that? Kind of a hot smell? Like something's burning?

## *Vision*

As the small line of students in front of him grew shorter, Kiprono felt increasingly ill at ease. It was not the strangers at the head of the queue that made him nervous – he had seen a few *wazungu* before, they did not frighten him. Once he got past the oddity of their pale limbs and faces he could accept them as harmless. No, it was the peculiar devices they held, the shiny metal objects they put up to the faces of the students ahead of him, that were the source of his discomfort. They looked painful, possibly dangerous. Despite what the headmaster had told the assembled children earlier that day – that the *wazungu* were here to take measurements from the eyes of certain students, that this was a good thing – he couldn't help feeling a little fearful. When at last it was his turn he almost bolted. Only the shame that would come from running away, the scorn that his classmates would heap upon him, kept him in place.

Kiprono's teacher, Miss Chebii, had noticed early on that he had difficulty seeing. From his desk a few rows back from the chalkboard he had to squint to make out what she had written – and then he usually got it wrong. Even after being moved to the front of the class

Kiprono struggled. So it was no surprise that his name went on the list of seven students to be examined by the group of whites visiting the village. These *wazungu* were not here as tourists; they were *daktari wa macho*, eye doctors, and they were going from village to village seeking out children with poor vision.

Kiprono held his breath and tried not to flinch as the *mzungu* lady put the strange device up to his eyes. Her Kenyan assistant instructed him when to say yes, when to say no. He tensed, but the pain he expected never came. He heard the white woman say softly "My, but you're a short-sighted little one," but the words held no meaning for him. In no time at all the examination was finished and Kiprono, drenched in relief, was sent back to his classroom. To his surprise and delight the other students regarded him with newfound respect and just a little awe.

At games time several of Kiprono's friends huddled around him, full of questions. When asked what had happened to him he was tempted to exaggerate but held back. He knew if he strayed far from the unremarkable truth the others who had been examined would be quick to put him in his place. A shy boy to begin with, Kiprono was not about to court disapproval and ridicule from his classmates.

Several weeks went by and the experience with the *wazungu* was all but forgotten. The topic of the new teacher from Nairobi now occupied front and center. The children – especially the boys – were shocked to see her wearing trousers around her house on the school compound at the end of the day. Some even wondered if she was really a man impersonating a woman – a silly notion that was put to rest by a boy who had once been to the capital city. Though his friends found it hard to believe, Kipkosgei insisted that many women there wore trousers and even shirts with no sleeves. And not just around their home but on the streets of the city, in full view of anyone. After that revelation, the behavior of Miss Wanjiku seemed much less bizarre – though the boys continued to stare.

One Friday morning, nearly a month after the foreign *daktari* had left, they returned. The students who had been examined were summoned to the headmaster's office, led into the adjoining staff room, and given their new eyeglasses. The doctors took a few minutes with each child, adjusting the *miwani* so that they sat just right on their small faces. Once satisfied with the fit, the five boys and two girls were sent back to class.

Kiprono strode proudly into the room – and was met by laughter. His heart sank to someplace near his feet. Nearly every one of his classmates was giggling or snickering, some mockingly held circled fingers up to their faces. Miss Chebii quickly lashed out at the class, angrily insisting they be quiet and continue with their reading lesson, but the damage had been done. Kiprono was devastated. He slouched down as far as he could in his chair and tried to hide his face from his peers. As discretely as possible he slipped the eyeglasses off his face and held them in his lap under the desk. The merciful sound of the lunch bell came none to soon.

As the other children filed out of the room, Miss Chebii discretely asked Kiprono to remain behind. Once the room was quiet, she took him aside. “Kiprono, you must not let the other children upset you,” she said kindly. “You should know that getting the *miwani* is a good thing, a privilege. You are a very bright boy, one of the best in Standard Three, and I know that you will do even better now that you have good eyes.” She added that, if he would promise to wear his glasses, she would move him to the back of the classroom, well away from the stares of the others. Kiprono reluctantly agreed. After carefully putting the *miwani* in his trouser pocket, he went outside to join the rest of the children.

After lunch he took his new seat – and was amazed. Though much farther from the board than before, he could make out Miss Chebii's writing quite clearly. There was no need to squint, no need to guess what certain letters really were. Not only that, everything else in the room seemed clearer, more distinct. He could see each individual hair curling at the base of Chepkiyang's thin neck, could make out the mole on Kipchumba's elbow – even though he sat in the front row! Only a few students turned round to look at him, and they were promptly scolded by Miss Chebii.

By the end of the school day Kiprono was feeling a strange mix of emotions: happy to have this sudden sharp vision, defensive toward his classmates, self-conscious about the strange apparatus perched on his nose, worried what his parents and siblings would have to say. Once out the door he ran straight home, sprinting ahead of the rest of the children. He had no desire to dally and be subjected to their teasing, away from Miss Chebii's protection.

At home, the critical reaction he had feared never materialized. His father did not say a word, just looked at him with pointed curiosity. His mother whispered a prayer of thanksgiving to both God and the *mzungu* doctors. Kiprono's two young sisters took turns trying the *miwani* on, wrestling them away from each other with such intensity he feared they would be broken. At the end of the evening Kiprono wrapped his new treasure carefully in a handkerchief, set it beside the bed, and tried to sleep.

Sleep was not about to come. He was far too excited about the events of the day to drift away. After tossing and turning for what seemed like hours, Kiprono got out of bed. He lit a small candle, hoping it would not wake his sisters, and put on his new glasses. After looking for a few minutes at the lesson in his exercise book he felt the need to go to the toilet and quietly slipped out to use the *choo*. Halfway there he looked up. An excited chill gripped him; he stopped dead in his tracks. Where before he had seen perhaps a dozen blurry white spots there were now hundreds – no, thousands – of brilliant points of light blazing brightly in the black sky. Dumbstruck, he sat down, a smile spreading quickly across his face. He was transfixed by the beauty of the stars, captivated by Orion, the Pleiades, the white smear of the

Milky Way, the myriad distant suns piercing the dark void of the night sky.

Kiprono lay back in the grass, held his breath, and let the universe envelop him.

## *Different*

I am not very smart.

I don't mean this as a joke. It's not funny to me, though I think it sometimes is to other people. I just mean that I'm not like everyone else. Nowadays the words to use when you talk about me are developmentally disabled. I like that better than retarded. I was retarded in school. Other kids would say it like it was something I'd stepped in. They would watch me, ready to laugh at anything I did that was different from what they would do. I hated that word. I knew I was different but I didn't want to be a retard. Who would?

You might not notice it at first but after a while you can see that I have trouble with money, with planning things in the future. Things my teachers called abstract thinking. I was told that part of my brain stopped growing while I was in my mother's stomach. I'm not so sure. I mean, how can anyone know that's what really happened? Why couldn't it have been something else, maybe something that happened to me when I was a baby? Then I could be angry at something I could point to, like maybe a fever I had or an accident where I hurt my head. To say it happened before I was born makes it sound like it was my mother's fault. It's not. She may be crazy, or at least she acts crazy, but I can't make myself blame her.

I was married once. She was a girl I knew from special ed classes in high school. We even went to the prom together, though neither one of us knew how to dance. Richard, he's my friend from way back, and also a special ed kid, kept trying to get us to dance. He said there was nothing to it, anyone can do it. I said no, I'll just look stupid and everyone will laugh at me. Okay 'fraidy cat, he said, I'll dance with Stephanie if you won't. And he did, even though she tried to get him not to. Just dragged her out on the floor and began moving around like he was having a seizure. All the regular kids started laughing at him, calling him spastic, spasmo, retard. Then he hit one of the guys who was calling him names and they both got kicked out. Stephanie was crying. I just wanted to hide in the corner and wait for everything to calm down. I did my best to look normal.

It seems like I'm better at that now that I'm grown up. I even have a few normal friends, nice people, a little older than me, mostly retired guys who don't mind being around me. We meet at the coffee shop a block away from my apartment every morning. At first they didn't know I wasn't the same as them (I can fool a lot of folks for a while) and now that they have been around me for some time they don't act bothered by it. Though I can tell sometimes when they talk to each other it's not exactly the way they talk to me, like they are less careful how they use their words when they think I'm not listening. Part of me feels a little angry, then I tell myself to calm down, they are looking out for me. And I can't really carry on a conversation like that anyway. I just don't think like they do, and I for sure don't have all the fancy words to throw around.

One of these guys, Alan, is always buying me coffee. I suppose he is my best friend. I think he feels like we have a lot in common, though really it's probably just that we both have epilepsy. We remind each other about our medicine, and I was there at the coffee shop when he had one of his seizures. I was pretty cool about it, too, I knew what was happening and put my coat under his head until the aid car arrived. By then he was over it and felt pretty embarrassed, but since then he has been really nice to me. I think if I ever need someone to help me in a bad situation, and I can't get hold of my sister, I would call Alan. He would know what to do.

Alan's girlfriend, though, is not very nice. Her name is Arlene and she likes to make fun of me. Not in a big way that Alan or the other guys would notice, but little things that get to me. Like when Alan got up to use the rest room and she saw one of my laces untied and asked me if I could tie it myself or did I need her to do it. Or how she raises her eyebrows when I say something that makes me sound smart (which I can do from time to time, especially if it involves the Seahawks or the Mariners). I try really hard to like her because of Alan but it's not easy. I'm just thankful she doesn't hang around Tully's a lot. I don't think she likes coffee all that much.

A couple of weeks ago I was in having a cup of coffee really early. I hadn't been able to sleep well and got bored watching TV in the apartment. I was just sitting there reading the comics in the newspaper when I looked up and saw Arlene walking past the window. I looked back down as quick as I could but it was too late, she saw me. When she came in and sat down next to me, rain dripping off her jacket onto the table and the newspaper sitting there, I got flustered. Alan wasn't there, she could be as rude to me as she liked. I waited for her to say something bitchy but she didn't, just smiled and said "Good morning, Jason" really friendly. Not like she usually talks to me. I looked down for a few seconds, and when I looked back up she was still smiling. Okay, I thought, this is strange. I said "Good morning" back to her then shut up and waited.

Arlene sighed and took off her jacket, hung it on a hook at the edge of the booth where it couldn't drip on us anymore. Then she looked me straight in the eye. "Alan tells me you don't have a girlfriend. Is that true?" She still sounded friendly, or maybe I just wanted her to be, I don't know. What could I do, though, I had to answer her. "No, not now, I like to keep my options open." I thought that was a smart way to answer her, but she threw another question at me, this time with a harder look in her eyes. "Have you ever had a girlfriend, would you even know what to do with one?"

That hurt. I felt hot and angry. It was hard to keep the tears out of my voice as I told her yes, I knew what to do, I had been married once, damn it. What made her think I didn't know how to have a girlfriend, how to be close to a woman? Maybe I was different from her and the others, but I wasn't *that* different. Then I leaned back in the booth and tried to get calm again. After a minute or so she reached over and touched my hand. "I'm sorry Jason, really I am. I didn't mean to make you upset. I was just curious. I don't really know that much about you, I was just trying to find out."

A few days later I got a call from Arlene. Alan had given her my number. She wanted to know if I would be at the coffee shop the next morning, she had someone she wanted me to meet. I probably took longer to answer her than I should have. Sure, I finally said, though I was feeling a little nervous.

I started to wonder what was behind her asking me. Just because she wanted me to meet someone didn't mean I was comfortable with the idea. And the more I thought about it the more uncomfortable I got. I could just stay home, I told myself, pretend I have the flu. There was a lot of it going around, everyone would understand. I couldn't bring myself to lie, though. Besides I was a little curious who this person would be. I was pretty sure it would be someone Arlene thought would make a good girlfriend for me, someone like me, a little slow, different. I couldn't decide whether to be irritated at her for thinking I couldn't have a normal girlfriend or be pleased with her for looking out for me. I gave up trying to figure it out and went to bed, though it took me a long time to fall asleep.

The next morning Arlene walked in the door of Tully's together with one of the prettiest women I had ever seen. Younger than me, probably in her thirties, with real pretty eyes and a big smile. Her name was Suzanne, she said, not Sue, she needed as big a name as she could to make up for being so short. Well, maybe she was short but not all that much. Mostly just small, tiny, kind of like a real life pixie with shiny black hair. And normal, definitely normal, smart in fact. You could just tell she was not like me. If I was nervous to start with it got much worse. I had no idea why Arlene had wanted us to meet, not now. My heart was pounding so loudly I almost didn't hear Suzanne when she asked me a question.

She asked a lot of questions, all about me and my life. Everyone else at the table was talking round and round about a lot of things, but Suzanne and I had our own private conversation. I liked the way she had turned her chair to look right at me, how she smiled as she talked, how she would touch my arm each time she had something else to ask me. Mostly it was about how I lived – did I work (no), was I widowed or divorced (divorced), had there been any children (none). How did I get around without a car? Was I able to make ends meet on my Social Security disability check? What did I do when I needed help with things that were hard to understand? She seemed happy that I knew how to use the bus system, had a little savings in the bank, and had a normal sister to help me through confusing or complicated situations. She was really nice and I couldn't help wanting to keep talking with her. After an hour we were the only two left at the table; everyone else had said goodbye and left, though I hardly noticed. I really didn't want us to stop talking, but it finally reached a point where we just sat and smiled at each other. I was definitely smiling by then. I was happier than I'd been in a long time. I wasn't even thinking when I blurted out that I would like to see her again, then sat back, my face turning red, afraid I had ruined everything. To my surprise she said she would like to see me again too, could she call me in a few days? Feeling tongue-tied all of a sudden I gave her my number. I couldn't believe my good luck.

***

I had spent the entire morning getting ready. I made sure the floor was swept and the counters were clean, had wiped down everything in the bathroom. The apartment was cleaner than it had been in weeks. I had gone to the store earlier for some good coffee, not the Folgers I drank at home. I really couldn't tell the difference but I was sure Suzanne could. She hadn't mentioned if she wanted to go out somewhere or have lunch at my apartment so I picked up some nice sandwich fixings and a couple of cans of what looked like gourmet soup. I was ready for her – and as nervous as I'd ever been.

The doorbell rang around noon. I was excited when I opened it and saw her there. Then I saw the guy she was with, standing behind her, a tall thin man with almost white hair. I wasn't so excited anymore. Something about him bothered me right off the bat. Maybe it was just the way he looked at me, sort of smirking like he was better than me. I had seen that look way too many times before.

Suzanne saw me staring at him and introduced him as her friend Matthew. Great, I thought, my face starting to burn. Bring your goddamm boyfriend with you! This was definitely not what I had imagined. I tried to be cool and invited them in. Matthew went right for the best chair in the room – actually it's the only chair in the room. It's big and comfortable. Suzanne sat down on my sagging couch. I joined her, sitting on the edge so I wouldn't slide down next to her. I was feeling really uncomfortable.

I think Suzanne could tell; she started talking about what a nice apartment I had, how she liked the tropical fish I had in the tank on the kitchen counter. Matthew cleared his throat and she stopped chattering. She looked at him, then at me. "Jason," she said, "I need to be honest with you. I didn't come here just to see you. I wanted you to meet Matthew. I think he is someone who can help you a lot. He's our *laibon*." Huh? I thought. What in the world is a LAY-bonn? I guess she could see I had no idea what she was talking about. "A *laibon* is a specially enlightened follower of *Sende*," she explained. "He has powers the rest of us aspire to, healing powers, deep insights." Okay, I thought, this is getting weird. What the hell is SIN-day? And why is it so important that I meet this guy? I must have spoken that last bit out loud because Matthew leaned forward in his chair and looked hard at me. It made me even more nervous the way he was staring, with that superior little grin of his. No matter what he said I had my mind made up to ignore it. I didn't like him.

"Jason, it's like this," he said, with a voice so soft I had a hard time hearing him. "*Sende* is a way of relating to life's primal energies, a way of becoming one with the world around us, both seen and unseen. I am blessed to be a *laibon*, to have had the all-powerful life force choose me when I was young. I have devoted my entire being to helping others elevate their consciousness, walked with countless men and women along the road to greater wisdom. I am a servant of all who wish to achieve greater insight, heightened perception." He smiled and sat back, looking happy with himself.

I was totally confused now. What was he talking about? He made me really uneasy, just like those holy rollers that come to my door from time to time trying to convert me. I looked at Suzanne. She must have known I was having a hard time understanding what he was saying because she smiled a big smile and asked me if everything was all right. No, I said, it wasn't. Who was this guy really? Was he a friend of Arlene's too? Actually, she said, looking embarrassed, Arlene and she weren't really friends. She just cut Arlene's hair. Arlene had told

Suzanne all about me and, well, she wanted to do something. And she really thought Matthew could help me.

I looked back at him sitting there smiling that weird little smile. “Okay,” I asked him, “what is it you think you can help me with?” “Intellectual growth, the expansion of mind skills, teaching your brain to transcend its current limitations.” He was going to keep on talking so I cut him off. “Why do you think I want any of that?” I asked. “Isn’t it obvious?” he answered. “You don’t have to pretend. I know you want to be normal, be just as smart as anyone else. I know you don’t want to be retarded.”

It was an hour after they had left and I was still pissed off. What a jerk. I had decided not to fix them lunch, didn’t even make coffee, just sat there angry, trying not to cry until Suzanne finally got the idea and stood up. “Please don’t make any hasty decisions,” she said as she stood at the door. “Just give him a chance. He’s really good. I think he can make a real difference in your life.” I wanted to give her a snappy reply but I couldn’t come up with anything. I just glared at her, ignoring Matthew entirely. When they walked away the asshole was still smiling.

After they’d been gone a while and I’d calmed down I got to thinking. What was this *Sende* stuff anyway? Was it for real – could Matthew really do what said he could? Did a *laibon* have that kind of power? I had no idea, but I wanted to find out. I called my sister and explained what had happened. She didn’t know any more about *Sende* than I did – which was nothing, really – but told me she would get on her computer and see what she could find out. I hung up the phone and waited.

I didn't have to wait long. About an hour later she called me back. It turned out there wasn't a lot on *Sende*, but what there was bothered her. Most of what she read wasn't good at all. *Sende* had started a while ago in some African country I'd never heard of, but caught on in Europe and America about the time the people back in Africa stopped believing in it. It was sort of a religion but without all the praying and church stuff. There were a lot of people complaining about how they had been tricked by it, how it was a joke. I found out that a *laibon* was a spiritual leader, sort of a witch doctor it sounded like. In Europe some families had sued a couple of *laibons* for taking their money and lying to them. That made me even more suspicious of Matthew. I thanked my sister; we both agreed I should be really careful around this guy.

That night I got a call from Suzanne. She sounded unhappy and said right away that she was sorry for how her visit had turned out. She hadn't meant to make me angry; she had just wanted to help, that was all. Would I think about what Matthew had said? Would I please give him a chance?

I had been waiting for this. Somehow I knew she would be calling me and I knew what I was going to do. Okay, I said, I'm willing to try. And if it doesn't work, if Matthew can't make me any smarter, would they just leave me alone? Yes, she agreed. But that wasn't going to happen. She knew he would be able to help me. He was going to make a big difference in my life. Fine, I said, I will give him a try. Too bad she couldn't see me smiling when I hung up.

***

Matthew lived a few miles from my apartment. I had to ask a couple of drivers for help, but I was able to get there on the bus. The stop was only two blocks from his place, and I didn't mind the short walk. It was a house just like the others in the neighborhood, not very fancy at all. The lawn had just been mowed and I worried about tracking grass into the house after walking up the sidewalk. When I rang the bell it wasn't Matthew who answered but an older woman, about my mother's age. She looked a little confused when I told her I was there to see Matthew, but she led me into the living room and left me alone. I wasn't sure what to do so I just sat there on the couch, looking around the room, waiting.

After a few minutes Matthew came in, wearing that same stupid smile. "It is so good to see you, Jason, so glad you decided to join me. I think together we can do some amazing things. The power of *Sende* is great." Yeah, I thought, let's see how great it really is. He led me into a back room with what looked like a long table, high off the floor, but padded like a big leather chair bottom. There were a bunch of crystals – those big clear, spiky things – underneath. I did as he said and climbed up on the table, lay on my back, and waited.

"Jason, we are going to start slowly today," he said in that irritating soft voice. "What you will feel this first session will be minor, but I think you'll notice a change right away. You will go away thinking a little more clearly, able to appreciate more complicated ideas. Let's get started." He turned the lights in the room down way low, lit a couple of strange smelling candles, and turned on some music. It wasn't like any music I'd heard before, sort of a funny moaning and whining with mostly soft drums in the background.

Matthew must have spent half an hour walking around me on the table, holding his hands a few inches above my body, never actually touching it. A lot of the time he spent doing weird motions, like little circles, then big ones, over my head. The whole time he was muttering words I didn't understand; I suppose they were some kind of African language but I really couldn't tell. I knew I was supposed to keep my eyes closed but I couldn't help myself and would sneak a peek every so often. Matthew was so wrapped up in whatever it was he was doing that he never noticed. He seemed like he was in some sort of trance. It was weird, but I didn't feel all that uneasy. I actually felt pretty calm; I almost fell asleep at one point.

Finally he was finished. He stepped back from the table, turned off the music, folded his hands, and told me to open my eyes. This was what I had been waiting for. I looked right at him and gave him my best dumb-as-a-rock, stupid moron look. I had practiced it in front of my bathroom mirror the day before until I got it down. It was a look I saw a lot of times on some of the other kids' faces, the ones who had it a lot worse than me, on the short bus back in school.

It worked; Matthew looked surprised and a little upset. "Jason, is everything alright?" he asked. I just stared. He asked me again; I kept staring. Finally, after he had started fidgeting and began moving closer to me, I opened my mouth. "Don't… Feel… Right," I said, talking real slow and acting like it was hard to spit the words out. Matthew stepped back away from me, looking worried. I kept it up. "Go… Home… Bus…" I said, keeping that stupid-ass look on my face. It was really hard to do; I had to keep from laughing and I sure didn't want to do that. I wanted him to squirm.

It took another few minutes but Matthew finally got the idea. I got off the table and started walking out into the living room, trying to look as confused as possible. When I got to the door he really got upset, ran in front of me to open it, then almost dragged me to his car. "I don't want you taking the bus in this condition," he said, almost yelling. I got in the passenger side and made a big show of trying to work the seat belt buckle. He was talking to himself a lot now, most of it I couldn't make out but I picked up on enough of the words to know he was really freaked out. It was all I could do to keep from smiling.

We got to my building and Matthew walked with me up to my apartment to be sure I could work the key and let myself in. Once I had the door open he practically ran away, hurrying down the stairs. I watched from my window and saw him peel out, almost running into another car as he left the parking lot. I let myself relax then, and started laughing so hard I worried my neighbors would hear me and complain. Although I didn't care if they did. I felt good, really good.

I kept waiting for Suzanne to call, but after three or four days I knew she wasn't going to. I was sure Matthew would never call. I stayed away from the coffee shop, though, just to make it seem more real that there was something wrong with me. In fact, I only left the apartment to get a few groceries, going to a store the opposite direction from Tully's. I wanted it all to seem real, mostly to Matthew and Suzanne, but also to Arlene. She was the one who started all this and I wanted her to feel a little bad about it. Alan called and left several messages. Arlene called once too and I could tell she felt bad; she sounded worried and wanted me to call her and tell her how I was doing. I didn't, of course. I was in no hurry.

Finally, when I thought I'd kept it up long enough, I showed up for morning coffee as if nothing had happened. Alan was there without Arlene (thank God) and he looked really relieved to see me. Where have you been, he wondered, was everything all right? We haven't seen you in over a week! Yeah, I told him, I was fine, just had a few days where I felt really weird and didn't want anybody to see me. Whatever had made me feel so odd was gone now. I could tell he was happy to hear this. He paid for my coffee and ordered me a cinnamon roll. We sat there and talked for at least an hour, mostly about the Seahawks and how they had surprised us in the playoffs. It felt good just to talk about normal things with someone who didn't care if I wasn't as sharp as he was. I was so happy that I had to get up and go to the bathroom so I could wipe my eyes. I didn't want anyone to see my tears; I just wanted to look as normal as the next guy. That's all I really want, anyway. I might not be smart but I'm not retarded.

And I'm sure as hell not stupid.

*In 1989 I contracted malaria while camping in the Kakamega Forest in Western Kenya. That same year I read George Alec Effinger's brilliant work,* Schrödinger's Kitten. *Together, those experiences inspired this story.*

*Effinger examined alternate, divergent futures that might spring forward from a single event. I chose to look backward instead.*

# *Parallel Lives*

He sat cross-legged at the edge of the forest, watching the mist rise from the tall grass on the meadow, listening to the early morning cries of the colobus monkeys in the canopy above. It started as a slight chill, nothing much, really, just a passing shudder. Still, best to be safe. He slipped back inside the tent and rummaged around for his sweater.

***

God, how he dreaded this. Walking in the door, dog tired and stressed out, looking forward to that first Scotch on the rocks, only to be met at the door by Sara, reminded of their (her) plans for the evening, barely enough time to grab a quick shower, pull on a clean shirt, toss down a furtive shot on the way out the door. And all just to spend the evening with a couple he didn't even like. Well, not exactly true – he did like Rachel, not without a certain amount of physical appreciation, maybe a spot or two of lust. She was a fine woman, even if a bit complicated for his taste. But David, her husband? A total waste, a man whose world was bounded by the like and familiar. A bore. He would try to talk of Africa, David would switch the subject to the stock market or how the Raiders were doing. He had never been east of Sacramento, south of Monterey. Why Sara enjoyed their company, had the patience to be Rachel's friend, eluded him. As they drove the few miles to their destination, wipers smearing the foggy windshield, the heater on full against the winter chill of the valley, he settled into a familiar defensive state, his mind slowly becoming blank, his expectations dialed down to floor level. Jeffrey knew it was going to be a long evening.

***

Rachel was there when he drove up, watched him climb out of the dusty jeep. He was smiling, it was a good weekend. He carried the tripod like a spear, waving it triumphantly in the air as he drew close. "I can't wait to show you Marble Canyon! Oh God, the second afternoon there I had a cloud break and a beacon of light hit the red wall. You won't believe it." He dropped the tripod, pulled her quickly toward him, enveloped her in a bear hug, gave her a quick kiss on the lips. Then, as if suddenly realizing it was her he was holding, a longer, more attentive one.

She loved seeing him this excited. It brought back what she most treasured of him, his exuberance, his fascination with visual beauty. She loved having him home. At least when he was like this.

While he brought in the rest of the gear from the jeep, Rachel finished the salad, turned the oven to broil, then waited. He would shower, he always wanted to get the dust of the desert off before he let himself relax, weary but wired from the eight hour drive. Why he was so in love with the desert, yet refused to live anywhere but alongside the Pacific, baffled her. He had tried to explain, but couldn't. It didn't matter. She could accept it even if she couldn't understand.

He came into the kitchen in a clean t-shirt and a pair of baggy shorts with way too many pockets, toweling dry his hair and beaming. This will be the best time, she told herself, before he settles in with a couple of IPAs and a full belly. "Jeffrey," she said tentatively, "I hope you don't mind but I made some plans for us, for after dinner. Not big plans, I know you're tired from the drive, from getting up early to beat the heat. It's just that David and Sara have been trying to connect with us for weeks and this is the one time we could all four be together. It won't be for long, I promise. I know how David grates on you, but we can skip out after an hour or two. We'll be home early, it won't even be dark until after we get to their place."

Jeffrey stopped toweling his hair, looked at her with a mix of irritation and resignation, then sighed. What the hell, he thought, it's only fair. I go off by myself anytime I want, why should I begrudge her an evening doing what she likes. Still, it was going to be a strain. He had to bite his tongue so much around David it bled. Thank God there was Sara to make up for it. He never grew tired of looking at her; she was the only reason he tolerated getting together with the Earlhams.

***

He woke deep in the night, blanketed in sweat. His forehead was in a vise, his bladder about to explode. Hurriedly unzipping the tent, he stumbled out into the cool moist air. Barely two meters away the chills caught him. He lurched frantically back into his nylon cocoon, burying himself under the light sleeping bag, tightening his body into a ball, shivering violently. Dawn was still hours away.

***

It was a gift of a day, the sun banishing the fog shortly after it rose, the sky an electric autumn blue, the sun warm on your neck while your ankles chilled in the shadows. Sara was off in Santa Barbara for a few days; her younger sister had separated and needed the advice and

and comfort of big sis. He had the place to himself and was living a full life in a few square feet of kitchen and back porch. Funny how simple his needs had become, a counterpoint to Sara's burgeoning embrace of suburbia. He ignored the complete set of china, the one she had gushed over when she found it in that overpriced Bay Area shop, and pulled an old plastic plate out of his neglected backpack in the garage. One pot to cook in, one fork to eat with, one plate to wipe clean with a damp paper towel. Life at its simplest.

The doorbell took him by surprise. Too late for a solicitor, not that many ever passed through this neighborhood. The mail had already been delivered. He opened the door with curiosity, was surprised to find Rachel standing there. She looked downcast, timid, completely out of character. He was taken aback. He was about to invite her in when she looked up, almost angrily. Before he could decide what to do next she was leaning into him, pressing her face against his chest. She started crying. Great, he thought, what do I do now? I'm no good at this sort of thing, why the hell couldn't this happen when Sara was here. He was still pondering the awkwardness of the situation when she looked up, wrapped her arms around his neck, and kissed him, hard, her teeth sharp against his lips. A brief eternity passed before he kissed her back.

***

The wine was fantastic, an amazing full-bodied red, too dark to see through, filling his nose with the heavy vanilla scent of oak. Just the right finish, encouraging him to take another sip to see if it would be as rewarding as the last. Rachel sat across from him, her auburn hair aglow in the late afternoon sun, smiling, her hand stretched across the table, resting on his arm. Looking at her he smiled back. This was a piece of heaven, snatched unexpectedly from a weekend of anticipated drudgery. They were supposed to be sharing a hillside cottage, overlooking the valley and its multitude of wineries, with David and Sara. The women had planned it long ago at the conclusion of a dinner when the men, awash in too much wine, felt unmotivated to resist. David seemed like he actually liked the idea. Jeffrey, on the other hand, would rather have spent the weekend pulling English ivy or sorting Rachel's incomprehensible laundry. But what could he do? The curse of marriage, he thought, is not so much compromise as the need to give in. At least once in a while.

They were supposed to meet at the cottage. The other couple should have been there well before them; David had control over his working hours and could leave early whenever he wanted. Jeffrey and Rachel arrived to empty rooms, went to the desk, learned that their friends would not be joining them. No explanation. Rachel tried calling but Sara did not pick up her phone. Something was amiss; Rachel was working herself up to a level of concern that alarmed Jeffrey. He excused himself to the balcony, knowing his wife would be calling again, and again. The bottle had just been opened when a relieved Rachel appeared beside him. "It's okay," she said, with a strange look on her face, somewhere between bewilderment and annoyance. "Sara's all right. She's leaving David."

The second bottle was nearly empty when it grew too dark to see the table in front of them. Jeffrey leaned over to kiss his wife, took her hand, and led them back inside, closing the glass door against the late spring chill.

***

His head still hurt, his clothes were sticky damp, but the chills were gone. A vague thickness had settled in his brain, thoughts had to force their way through a layer of wet gauze. He knew something was badly wrong, but the obvious explanation made no sense. He had taken his chloroquine religiously, had made sure the insidious parasite would find no welcome within his body. It must be something else, something that mimicked malaria, some unknown malady he was ill-equipped to deal with, He had to move, that was obvious; he needed to work his way out of the jungle and into town. If the chills and fever stayed at bay he might make it all the way to the road today. If not, then as far as the forest station. No need to pack up the tent then, just leave the camp where it was. He could come back for everything once he was over the fever. Soon. It would be soon.

***

Jeffrey sat in the waiting room, staring at the year old *New Yorker*, unable to focus long enough to make it through a single paragraph. A few yards away, separated by plaster, dark glass, a maze of pipes and whirring machinery was his lover, the core of his life. The doctors had explained it calmly, reassuringly. Sara had suffered a stroke, not a massive one thank God, but big enough that she would be away from her everyday world for several weeks, maybe longer. She would need therapy to regain normal speech, to move about simply where she had floated gracefully before. His lithe, feline Sara would walk with ponderous deliberation for weeks, perhaps months. He didn't mind, not for himself. He was happy just to have her alive; limitations were the least of his worries. It was her own reaction he painfully anticipated, how she would strain against the limits of muscle, tongue, brain. He told himself she would recover, he didn't doubt for a moment her tenacity, her will to succeed. But what if she couldn't triumph? What if she were doomed to a life lived in a prison of physical restriction? What if? He stared once again at the unread magazine in his hands.

Rachel came quickly into the room, rushed over to Jeffrey. She wrapped her arms around him just as David came through the door. "Oh God," she moaned, "Will she be okay? Is she going to recover?"

Jeffrey looked at the door to Intensive Care, imagining his Sara passive on the bed, tubes and wires sprouting from her body. He closed his eyes, pulled away from Rachel's arms. Word-like sounds caught in his throat as he strode out the door, through the hall, and ran down four flights of stairs into the night.

***

He had not been able to get out of bed for days, trapped by the shimmering orange heaviness that bound him to the damp mattress, barely able to lean over and piss in the dented aluminum pan beside the bed. The room smelled thick, fetid. His body was on fire, the pain in his head a familiar constant. He was vaguely aware of the time – the afternoon it was, had to be from the warm light on the far wall. Slowly he became aware that he was waiting, but for what he couldn't recall. The dream was all he was sure of, the drifting on swells of alertness followed by the sudden plunge into near darkness. It was familiar by now. And he no longer had to piss.

It was in one of the lucid moments that she found him. Rachel had played a hunch, knew after he didn't show for three days that he had never left the forest, else he would have made it out to the road, found a working telephone, explained his delay. If he were sick he would have holed up in the old forest station, a small decaying house perched atop wooden stilts. She could find it easily enough, planted on the edge of a clearing surrounded by a thick African tangle of tree and vine. She felt certain he would be there. And he was. Jeffrey was too responsible to venture out in the thick of a fever. He knew enough to stay put.

She listened as he described the course of his illness, as best he could determine it, the cyclical interplay of fire and ice, the sweating, the shivering. Malaria. He had been like this for days, had to be incredibly dehydrated. He had only stayed alert and vocal for a few minutes. Now he had slipped away, unresponsive save for a gentle shivering. This was not good. She tried to get him to take some water, but all she succeeded in doing was wetting the front of his grimy shirt. She knew at once: she had to get him out of here, had to get liquids and antimalarials into his body as quickly as possible. The parasites coursing through his bloodstream could find their way to his brain at any time. Cerebral malaria. She wouldn't allow herself to mouth the words, she had to concentrate on logistics.

From the road to the forest station had taken her a good two hours, walking steadily on an uphill path, snaking deeper into the green darkness. She was not a large woman, she couldn't carry him, and he was in no condition to travel under his own power. She thought a bit then bolted from the house, searching frantically around the area, looking for something. An axe. A blade. Some way to cut a pair of saplings, strip some bark for twine to bind them. Nothing, not an object anywhere near her that was sharper than her own teeth. There was no way she could construct a travois, slide him slowly downhill to the road. The only solution she had come up with, her one best hope, was an impossibility. Rachel's spirits sagged.

She would have to go for help, hike back down to the road, wait however long it took for a vehicle to come by, try to get to Kongoro and find a chemist. Get Fansidar and as much bottled water as she could carry. Saline and an IV needle if she could get them. And get back in time. She did not dwell on the last concern.

Rachel hurried back to the house, hoping to find him coherent, to explain her leaving him for the moment. As she passed through the door the harsh certainty hit her in the gut. She felt the nausea rising, fell over her own feet the short distance to his bed. He had rolled onto his side, was looking at her, smiling, his crooked front teeth glowing luminously from between his cracked lips. He looked slightly puzzled, quizzical, as if he were just figuring out a conundrum. He looked tired, he looked old, he looked horribly out of place in this dank, musty place.

She stared into his unblinking eyes, hoping for recognition, finding none. At length she looked away, out through the open door where the afternoon shadows were tickling the edge of the clearing, where sunbirds were flitting from blossom to blossom. She could hear the colobus noisily stirring, the mechanical clatter of hornbills' wings as they passed through the forest, the harsh pounding of her own heart. She looked one last time at the man on the bed beside her.

He didn't look at all like Jeffrey.

## *Hand Lake*

He woke, suddenly alert, listening. Waiting. Nothing, just the pounding of his heart, the blood rushing in his ears. After several minutes he relaxed, convinced himself it was his imagination, probably just the harsh beginning of a dream. He snuggled deeper into the thin bag, thankful for the meager warmth of the tent, for the nearly windless night. He felt himself drifting back into sleep, was slipping into the calm nether world waiting there. At the moment he began to fall off the cliff of consciousness he jerked upright.

The sound was there, quite a ways away, barely audible. His pulse quickened, he felt the muscles along his spine tighten. Whatever it was it sounded like it was coming closer. Slowly. He couldn't place it, had no idea what – or who – was approaching the tent. He waited, struggling to keep fear from gaining a foothold. Listening. It was definitely coming closer.

He had intended to make it over the pass by late afternoon, was hoping to be in Sisters, or at least as far as Cold Springs campground, before dark. It was soon apparent that was not to be. A late start, coupled with an unexpected flurry of wet snow, had him beginning the climb shortly after noon. It had been a long hard slog up Deadhorse Grade – he was in far worse shape than he'd anticipated, was struggling through each tight uphill curve, thighs aching, lungs burning, the taste of copper pennies in his throat. He had taken to riding in the middle of the road, trying to save energy by cutting switchbacks, something he could only do this early in the season. Toiling away in his bottom gear, moving scarcely faster than he could walk.

The snow gates were still closed, not a car anywhere on the road on this chilly April afternoon. When the chain broke, and he had to waste precious time repairing it, he knew he was in trouble. By the time the grade began to level it was growing dark. When he saw the trail leading off to the north, to a small lake he'd never noticed before, he knew he had no choice. He pushed the heavy bicycle a few hundred feet, found a mostly level place to camp, and hurriedly pitched the tent. After a simple meal of granola bars and a banana – not enough energy to fuss with the small stove he was carrying – he turned in. The chill of the altitude was more than he had bargained for. Morning was a long way off.

He was on edge now, trying his best to quell a rising fear. The noise, a snuffling, grunting sound punctuated by muffled clanging, was unearthly, nothing he had heard before. Soon it would be at the tent, his options gone. He fumbled in the dark for his flashlight, for anything he could use as a weapon. His hand found the flimsy metal tire pump, a thin aluminum tube. No real advantage in a fight but it was all he had. He took a deep breath, summoned what courage he could muster, and quickly threw open the tent flap. With an awkward lurch he was out into the moonless night, his makeshift staff clenched menacingly in one hand, fumbling to switch on the light with his other.

As he rapidly swept the beam across the ground in front of him he paused – then exhaled loudly, began shivering with relief, convulsed with barely restrained laughter. There, a few yards from the tent, was a skunk. Its head stuck in a discarded tin can, it was blindly snorting and banging against whatever rocks and branches lay in its path.

Slowly, quietly, he slipped back into the tent and the welcoming sleeping bag, listening as the unfortunate creature moved past the tent and deeper into the underbrush. By the time it was out of earshot he was dead to the world.

## *Theft*

As soon as he walked through the door Peter knew something was wrong. It was nothing he could put a finger on, though, just a strong sense of being not right. He looked around the room but came up blank; things were still in order, nothing unusual caught his eye. Oh well, he thought, I'm just tired. School has really taken it out of me lately. He moved to the corner of the house that served as his kitchen, shook the almost empty gas canister, and lit the water for tea. After the kettle had boiled and he had set the tea to steep he returned to the main room to wind down his day with the BBC news. It was then he noticed his short wave was missing.

The small radio was his link to the world outside the village, a news source more relevant than the outdated Kenyan newspapers that littered the staff room. He listened to it most evenings, found that it helped him escape the confines of his current reality. Cursing under his breath, he reflected on his naïveté. He had been told, shortly after arriving in Kaprop, that theft was unheard of among the Kalenjin, that a locked door was an insult, a sign of mistrust of his neighbors, his community. And true, he had gone away twice before on school holidays with his doors left unsecured and nothing had gone missing. That did nothing to quell his current agitation, his rising anger. Grabbing his flashlight he burst out the door and hurried back uphill to the school to inform Kipruto, the headmaster.

There were suspects. Earlier that day a young man and his older companion, a local drunkard, had been in the school compound. In hindsight their presence seemed suspicious. They had come to his door with an unusual complaint. The young man was known to Peter. His name was Christopher – criss-TOFF-er was the local pronunciation – and he should have been in Form IV. His family had no money for school fees, however, so he fended for himself as best he could. Peter had been warned early on not to trust him, that he was, in the words of the headmaster, a "boy of some delinquent tendencies". The youth's grim demeanor and grimy clothes did nothing to defeat that conception.

Peter had not given the pair's story much credibility. It had to do with a dead civet that some of his boys had proudly displayed the day before. Christopher maintained that the cat was his, not the property of the Wildlife Club students who were claiming it as their own. He had killed it, not them. They had ganged up on him, stolen the creature from him. He implored Peter, the patron of the club, to set the matter straight. Peter had listened halfheartedly, not entirely understanding the situation, then sent the two away to tell their tale to the headmaster.

The pair were accosted inside the village bar and quickly escorted back to the compound by the school's *askari* and a few of Peter's fellow teachers. Once inside, they were locked in a storeroom adjacent to the headmaster's office. Within minutes a group of five or six of the village elders arrived, along with another dozen or more onlookers. Peter recognized most of the *wazee*, was casual friends with a couple of them. The seriousness with which his complaint was being taken made him uneasy.

The door to the storeroom was opened and the whimpering man led out. The small crowd of onlookers – mostly students – erupted into and jeers and derision. To Peter's shock and dismay, they were laughing and taunting him, screaming "I want your heart", "I want your liver", "I will tear off your arms". He felt sick at heart – how was this possible, how could his smiling, well-behaved students behave this way? This was not Nairobi, where a cry of "stop, thief!" could lead to a fatal beating. How could this be happening here, in his own small village?

As he passed by, reeking of *busaa*, the *mzee* looked at Peter with pleading eyes. "*Mimi si mwizi*," he said, I am not a thief. Peter looked away.

The old man was quickly stripped to his underwear by a trio of elders and dragged protesting into the staff room. There, under the harsh glare of a hurricane lantern, he was spread face down over the table while

Francis Kipchumba, the village sub chief, poured water over him. Grabbing a freshly cut cypress branch, Kipchumba started beating the man hard on the back, swinging with both hands from high overhead. Huge welts rose immediately; the man cried out in pain.

Peter was shocked, shouted for the beating to stop. As he stepped forward Kipruto grabbed his hand, jerking him around. "*Usisemi!*" The headmaster hissed. "Do not speak!" He led Peter quickly to a far corner of the room. "This is not your *shauri*," he said, his voice a strained whisper. "This is for us to deal with. It is a crime against the school, against Kaprop. We will deal with this in our way."

Taken aback, Peter swallowed his outrage and watched, helplessly. After several minutes the beating stopped. Guilty or not, the *mzee* had not confessed. His pleading had convinced his judges. "He is not the guilty one," Kipruto confirmed.

After the old man was returned to the storeroom they brought out Christopher. The youth was expressionless, looked blankly at the crowd of taunting, laughing boys, at the *wazee* surrounding him, at Peter. When he was taken into the staff room Peter could not make himself follow. He stood meekly outside the door, hearing the slap of branch on wet skin, straining in vain to hear any sound from the boy on the table.

At last it was finished. Christopher had not said a word, had not cried out. Of course not, Peter told himself, he must be used to this, used to being treated poorly. Especially by those boys who could afford to attend school, his superiors. His silence, his refusal to admit to any wrongdoing, was to be expected – and would convince his tormentors of his guilt. Peter watched as the *wazee* led the youth back to the storeroom, then turned and walked slowly back to his house.

A week went by with no word on the case, no confession, no recovery of the radio. At the start of the second week Peter was summoned to the police station in Tambach, a journey that would chew up an entire day. He needed to file a formal complaint, to witness against Christopher who had still not confessed. Irritated, he cancelled his classes, knowing he would be letting his Fourth Form boys down. Exams were only a few days away, and the stress they felt was palpable. He had no choice, really. He just wanted the episode over, finished. At this point he didn't even care about the damned radio. Just get the kid to own up to the theft and be done with it.

It was a two-hour ride by *matatu*, packed like a sardine with a dozen locals in the back of a small pickup truck, the smell of sweat, wood smoke, and *busaa* bringing him close to nausea. When he pulled himself out of the bush taxi in front of the police station the two officers on duty were perplexed. Why was an *mzungu* riding in public transport? Why not just drive his car? Peter tried to explain: he was not a wealthy expatriate, he was a Peace Corps Volunteer, this was how he traveled. His audience was clearly skeptical. To hell with them, he thought, just take me to Christopher and get this over with.

"We have tried to get a confession," one of the officers explained, "but he is not cooperating. He is very stubborn, that one." Peter nodded. "You should speak with him, perhaps he will obey you." I doubt it, Peter thought, but agreed to meet with Christopher.

After waiting a few minutes in a barren room behind the station, the young man was led in, handcuffed. His face and arms were covered with bruises, his lip split. He looked terrified, staring at the floor, avoiding Peter's gaze.

Peter's gut clenched. He had hoped he could get Christopher to own up to the theft; now he had serious doubts. Why would someone endure beatings over something as insignificant as a small radio? Why would he let himself be treated that way when a simple confession would make it all stop?

Christopher looked up at last, staring at Peter through the one eye that wasn't swollen shut.

"Christopher, why will you not admit to what you did? If you do the police will stop beating you"

"*Mwalimu*, I did not take your *nini*," Christopher mumbled, once again staring at the ground.

"I don't believe you!" Peter said, almost shouting. "Why do you keep denying it? If you will just confess this will all be over."

Silence. A minute, maybe two passed. Neither spoke. At last, Peter tried a different approach.

"All right, if you didn't take the radio then who did? Was it the old man?"

"No *mwalimu*. He did not take it. He drinks much, but he is not a *mwizi*. Those boys, they want to punish me."

"And why is that, Christopher?"

"Because I am not like them, *mwalimu*."

A few days after his trip to Tambach, a fellow teacher stopped by to let Peter know that Christopher had been released. The police had finally given up on extracting a confession, were unable to find the stolen radio. They had simply thrown the young man out of the station, leaving him to find his way back to the village with no money, no friends. A full day's walk, much of it steeply uphill.

The teacher had more news. That same afternoon the *wazee* had approached Father O'Connell, the priest who traveled the area. They were very much troubled at the lack of progress uncovering the thief, and felt the time had come to play the strongest card in their hand. They would curse the wrongdoer. And, in order to get the greatest effect from the curse, they proposed to do the cursing inside the small church on the school compound. Clearly Jesus would want the wrong made right. Adding his power to the curse could only help.

The priest thought a bit, then offered a compromise. He could not allow such a thing to take place inside the church. But surely it would not be a problem if the elders pronounced their curse on the church steps. The *wazee* found this a very favorable solution and began the ceremony with somber formality.

One evening, a few days after the cursing, Kipruto came to Peter's house. He was holding the radio. The headmaster stood awkwardly in the doorway until Peter urged him inside, remained ill at ease as tea was prepared. Once they were sitting, cups in hand, he shared what he had learned. The thieves were not the two original suspects. The radio had been recovered in Eldoret, the market town a few hours' travel from the school. A friend of the culprits had become frightened for their safety, worried sick about the curse brought down upon them. He had led one of the *wazee* to the shop where the radio had been sold.

So who were the thieves, Peter asked. Kipruto shifted uncomfortably in his chair and looked to the side as he spoke.

"They are two of your students."

Peter's surprise quickly turned to outrage, he struggled to contain his anger. "My students? *Kweli*? Which ones?"

When the headmaster spoke their names, it was as if he had been kicked in the groin. Stephen Rotich and Philip Cheserem. Two of the brightest boys in Form III, outspoken, rather sophisticated young men. Peter liked them, enjoyed their contributions to classroom discussions, appreciated their spirit. Both were from Nairobi, Kipruto explained, had been sent to live in the countryside by their families. Their parents were worried that they would lose their moral compass in the city, were certain they would benefit from being in a more traditional community. The irony was not lost on Peter. Urban kids, they probably looked at their surroundings as vulnerable, his unlocked door as an invitation. So much for embracing traditional values.

So, asked Peter, what will become of them? Will they be punished? Expelled?

Kipruto looked even more uncomfortable. "No, *mwalimu*, they will not be expelled. Their parents are from this place, they give much money to the school, to the community. Their families are important, everyone knows of them. They own many cows, have very large *shambas*. But yes, the boys will be punished. They must do hard work around the compound during preps time for the rest of the term. And they will not be allowed to take part in athletics on games days. The *wazee* agreed that that would be their proper punishment."

Peter was livid, caught himself swearing aloud. That's all, he thought? That's considered punishment? He recalled the two boys the night of the theft, how they had been at the front of the swarm of students surrounding Christopher and the old man, how they had been laughing and yelling at the two. He thought of Christopher in jail, the beatings, the humiliation. It was too much to deal with at the moment, his emotions were raw, his mind racing. "You must go now," he told Kipruto, "I need to think on this. We will talk tomorrow."

The following morning Peter stopped by the staff room before school and told his colleagues he would not be taking classes that day, that he was going to the mission to speak with Father O'Connell. The silence in the room buoyed his determination to seek support, a word of advice from someone outside the school, the village. Someone who was not of this place, who might offer counsel, perhaps help him find a way to make the thieves pay the proper price for their actions. Someone more like him.

It was a long, dusty walk along the escarpment road to Malawa Mission. Normally Peter found it pleasant, enjoyed the view of the valley below, the smiling exchanges with farmers working their fields, the pleasant bantering with the myriad *watoto*, too young for school, who lined the road to watch the *mzungu* pass by. Today he stared straight ahead, not speaking a word, ignoring those who hailed him. The anger he harbored showed no sign of lessening. After the better part of two hours he found himself knocking on the mission door, was greeted by Matthew, the cook and handyman. Yes, Father O'Connell was there, in fact he was expecting Peter. Word had traveled faster than Peter could walk – something he had found amusing in the past. Today he was not amused.

The good Father beckoned to join him. Once Peter was sitting, sinking low in an ancient leather chair, he felt deflated. "Father, I don't know whether to fight or just give up. How can I look at those two, let alone have them in my class? Why can't they be expelled? Back home there would have been no question, none at all. They would have been kicked out straight away."

"Ah yes, but you are not back home. Things are done differently here."

Peter bristled. He knew damned well that he was an outsider, a guest. Yet he had heard over and over again how much the Kalenjin despised theft, how stealing was an act not committed against a person but against the entire community. If they truly believed that, why give the perpetrators such a mild slap on the wrist?

"So I should just keep quiet, act as if everything is okay? Pretend I'm satisfied with their punishment?"

"Yes, Peter, it is not your *shauri*. That is exactly what you should do. The *wazee* have made their decision. Now, shall we have a beer?"

The next day Peter stood in the doorway to the Form III classroom, waiting, greeting his students as they passed in solemnly, one by one. At last, just moments before the bell, Rotich and Cheserem arrived. Peter moved forward to meet them.

"You are not welcome in this classroom, not while I am teaching. Go! See the headmaster, tell him to find something useful for you to do. I wash my hands of you." With that he turned and strode through the door, slamming it behind him.

At lunch break the staff room was quiet, none of the good-natured chatter that ordinarily filled the small space. All eyes were on Peter as he filled his bowl with *ugali* from the pot, put a small amount of *sukuma wiki* on top, and walked out the door. He had no stomach for companionship, not today. He found a quiet place under a tree at the edge of the compound, away from everyone else, and sat down to pick at his meal.

He had been there for only a few minutes when he noticed a familiar figure walking along the dirt path that bounded the schoolyard, growing closer. A short man, a boy really, leading a goat on a tether. As he grew nearer Peter recognized him – it was Christopher. He felt flushed, agitated. He pulled himself back around the trunk and sat still, hoping the youth would pass him by unnoticed.

Christopher was almost past him when the goat stopped to snatch at a tuft of grass near Peter's tree. He looked up, met Peter's eyes with his usual sullen stare. Peter stood; Christopher tensed, looked as if he were about to run. "Christopher," Peter said, "please don't go. Don't be angry with me. I was fooled – we all were cheated – by those boys. I am sorry I did not believe you."

Christopher continued staring, though he no longer seemed about to flee. His grim face belied no emotion.

"I mean it," Peter continued, "I am very sorry. I wish I could have stopped the *wazee* from caning you, could have kept the police from beating you. I wish I had known. I should have believed you. *Niliamini uongo*."

To Peter's surprise, a grin slowly crept across Christopher's face. Then a smile. "*Mwalimu*, it is not a problem. I am fine now. The *wazee* gave me this goat!" With that, the youth tugged hard on the rope, jerking his prize into step behind him, and trod down the dusty path.

Peter waited until he was out of sight, then got up slowly and walked back toward the staff room, past the classrooms, entered his small house. It took him less than twenty minutes to pack his duffel, to take the few things he needed – some clothing, his razor, a book or two – and a few others that would bring memories of this place.

By mid-afternoon he was on the village *matatu*, bound for Eldoret, there to catch a bus to Nairobi. He was done, finished with Kaprop, already plotting how he would plead with the Peace Corps office to find him a new posting. He was strangely at ease, felt the tension of the past few weeks easing.

A few hours later the bus passed by Lake Naivasha. The setting sun cast long shadows across the plain, giraffes were browsing acacias on the lakeshore. Peter looked out the window and smiled, felt himself starting to doze. As he was nodding off he realized he had left the radio on the table.

## *Longing*

You reach for my hand
slowly, demurely
our fingers intertwine
I cannot stop the smile from forming

*Be still, careful now, others are watching*

Touching you, discretely, chastely
careful not to draw attention
when what I desire is to hold you
bury my face in your hair
feel your body's heat through our embrace
wake in your arms

*I fill your wine glass, you look up and smile*

We talk obliquely, abstractly, conjure fantasy scenarios
that will never be ours to explore
yet alluring, intriguing

*In another life we would be lovers*

I would lead you by the hand into a hut on Lamu
sand clinging to our feet, our calves, our thighs
the evening wind singing through the palm thatch
the air cooling now, the sun low over the ocean

the moon yet to rise
We would wake before the sky grew bright
walk the beach in the moonlight,
looking east, imagining Arabia off the far horizon
You would lean against me, your head on my shoulder
We would stop, laze on the warm white firmament
and wait, patient, not hurrying,
knowing the dawn awaits us
ours to share

*I would slowly undo your top, unwrap your skirt,*
*ease you down on the warm ground*
*covering you with kisses*

The call to prayer would rouse us,
we would walk back to the edge of town
to a small *hoteli* where the sleepy owner
would serve us *chai* spiced with cardamom
and *mandazi* hot from the *jiko*
Trying to be neat
you would lick the oil from your fingers
and playfully smear my forehead
I would laugh and hold you once more
knowing my life could never be richer
than at this one moment

## *The Author*

Stephen Mustoe is a writer and photographer. He grew up in a small town north of Seattle and graduated from Harvard College and the University of Oregon. After a stint with the Peace Corps in Kenya in his mid-thirties, he returned home to embark on a career as a high school teacher, a vocation that captured his heart and energies for twenty years.

An inveterate traveler, Mustoe has trekked the Himalayas of Nepal several times, knocked about from village to village in East Africa, bicycled across the United States, and twice motorcycled solo from Oregon to northernmost Alaska. He lives in Eugene, Oregon, with his wife and four cats.